D0366026

The Heirs of the
MEDALLION
BOOK ONE

ADZUL

David Sage

Pia,
Best wishes

The Heirs of the Medallion
Copyright © 2013 by Mr. Sage's Stories

For information about this title or to order other books and/or
electronic media, contact the publisher:
Mr. Sage's Stories
mrsagesstories.com

ISBN: 978-0-9894210-0-3

Printed in the United States of America

Cover and Interior design by: 1106 Design

Table of Contents

With Thanks

TO MY THREE CHILDREN, David, Tierney, and Tyler, whose need for distraction as youngsters, during long backpacking trips, led to the inspiration for telling stories. Decades later, your encouragement and inspiration have made this book possible.

To teachers and administrators, among them Leslie, Jean, Gay, and Lis, in dozens of schools, who have asked me to return time after time through the years. You kept my avocation alive when other activities could have distracted me.

To thousands of kids who wanted another story from "Mr. Sage." Your excitement kept me coming back!

To my sister Robin, whose request for a tale to the students of Center, Colorado about cultural heritage led to the creation of this story.

Finally, to my wife Marcia for her support and enthusiasm during my countless trips to schools and the many, many hours it took to create this book. I love you.

David Sage
Story, Wyoming

CHAPTER 1

Ears

Blood was pouring out of a deep sword wound in the dying man's neck. It began to trickle from his mouth, but the words kept spilling out as he stared into the eyes of the warrior holding him. Oblivious to the shouts and screams of the battle around them, the younger man bent his head close as the voice began to fade.

"You must leave, my son. They have finally found Pattiti and they will kill every man, woman, and child in their search for gold." With enormous effort he lifted one hand to a braided leather strap around his neck. "Take the medallion. You must wear it for as long as you live." He coughed and more blood ran from his

1

mouth. "It will warn you of danger and protect you," he said as his voice trailed off.

With great gentleness, the warrior lifted the strap from his father's neck and pulled the large, round piece of silver attached to it from under the bloody armor shirt. It was 3½ inches across, with a 1-inch square hole in the middle. Distinctive marks were cut into the surface on both sides. He slipped it around his own neck, noticing as he did so that the silver was strangely hot.

The older man's eyes closed for a moment but he rallied. "I served the Emperor, now you must serve the people. But you have to leave the Empire. Escape to the north; find a friendly race. Live with them and take care of the medallion. It possesses a great secret. Some day a member of our family will discover it. Until that time, it is to be passed on to the youngest member of the family when the wearer is old and near death. Do you understand?"

"Yes, father. But the Incan people need me right now to fight for them!"

"No!" The older man exerted all his strength, lifting his head and speaking clearly. "You will be killed by the Spaniards if you stay! The family has a more important mission; the medallion must be preserved! Promise me that you will go!"

In the face of such intensity, the son knew that he must obey. "You have my word, father. I will go."

The head slumped forward, eyes closed. The young man thought that death had come, but the eyes fluttered open and the voice went on, barely a whisper. "Teach your children and their children to use the sling and to weave the armor shirts. The family must honor this tradition until the secret is discovered."

"Yes, father."

"Now, go!" With a slight shudder, life went out of his body.

The warrior carefully lowered his father's head to the ground. For a moment he remained on one knee before scooping a sling from the pavement and leaping to his feet. The cacophony of battle engulfed him and he realized that the warriors had been forced back to within a few yards of where he stood. They were engaged in hand-to-hand combat with soldiers in metal armor. Dead and dying from both sides were being trampled underfoot as the conflict raged over them.

A warrior nearby glanced back and saw the dead man and the medallion hanging around the neck of the son. "Run, Adzul!" he bellowed. "Your father told us that he was passing on to you his role of servant to the Empire. You must not stay and be killed!"

"In a moment," shouted the young man, eyes searching the battle. Over the heads of the struggling men, he could see a few horsemen wielding swords and lances. One in particular stood out. He had a metal helmet, thin face, and a pointed black beard. His eyes were cruel and he swung a sword from his plunging horse, smiling as an Incan warrior went down under the blow. It was the Spanish captain.

All the rage and grief over his father's death boiled up as Adzul plucked a rock from the pouch at his belt and loaded the sling. In an instant, the 5-foot straps were spinning around his head in a blur. The rock was released and another loaded with blinding speed.

The captain paused to search for his next victim. In that moment, the first rock grazed his left cheek and tore the left earlobe completely off his head! Blood poured down his neck. Clapping his hand over the bloody hole, the captain screamed in pain and anger, only to feel his right earlobe severed like a knife by the second rock! With both hands to his head, blood running between the fingers, the Spaniard roared with rage, looking for the assailant. Just behind the Incan battle line he saw a lone warrior look directly at him, smile broadly, and take off running.

The captain was blind with fury. An arrogant man, he knew people would whisper and laugh behind his back at this deformity until the day he died. "Capture that man and bring him to me" he shouted above the battle noise, pointing both bloody hands at the Incan disappearing around the corner of a building. "Five pieces of gold to the man who brings him back alive!"

CHAPTER 2

The Medallion

THE STORYTELLER PAUSED, eyes closed as he imagined the scene. He was very old — 100 years in fact, with skin the color of deeply polished leather. But his body belied his age. It was slender and trim, clad in a blue denim shirt and jeans. Strong hands and roughened boots revealed his capacity for work. To tell the truth, no one in the town of Center, Colorado spent more hours in their vegetable garden than he. No one produced a finer crop. No one could match the cash customers that came to his door!

It was 8:00 on the morning of June 21, 1993, the summer equinox. The weather was perfect: 80 degrees and not a cloud in the sky. The porch at the front of his small white house was festooned with hanging pots of petunias, geraniums, and pansies. On a couple of tables, set carefully back from the sun, pots of impatiens boasted pale purples and whites.

He sat in a beautiful rocking chair at the side of the front door. It was made of cherrywood, and he had carved every piece many years before. It was held together by wooden dowels, no nails or screws had been used. At his feet, two kids sat cross-legged. They were twins, 12 years old. Both had black hair, brown eyes and brown skin. If it weren't for the shoulder-length hair and blouse on the girl, one couldn't have told them apart.

Earlier that morning, at sunrise, the three of them had stood in his front yard as the sun rose over the Sangre de Cristo Mountains to the east. From around his neck he had pulled a large piece of silver. It was circular, with strange markings carved on it and a square hole in the middle.

"Look through the hole at the sun as it rises above the peaks and tell me what you see," he said, handing it to the kids.

"What do you mean, Great Grandfather? What are we supposed to see?" asked Juan, fingering the strange piece, as he and Sophia put their heads together to look through the hole.

"We see the trees and houses across the street," his sister declared.

"You may see nothing. Wait until the sun is clear of the highest peak and then tell me," the old man replied.

Ever so slowly the sun emerged above the jagged heights of snow-covered rock. As it cleared the last one, there was a sharp intake of breath from the twins and Juan raised his head to look over the silver. Bending again to look through the hole, he almost shouted, "It's gone! The town is gone! There's nothing but smoke!"

"Wait," his sister's voice was hushed. "It's clearing!"

"What do you see?" Great Grandfather's voice was almost a whisper.

"Buildings, white buildings with enormous mountains behind them. A paved square place surrounded by the buildings. Men. Two kinds of men. Some are white, with black beards. They seem to be old-fashioned soldiers in armor; a few are on horses. The others are brown skinned, they are wearing sandals and loincloths, they have headbands with two feathers sticking up in front in a 'V,' and they have whitish shirts. They look like warriors." Sophia spoke rapidly.

"Wait," Juan interrupted, "they're starting to fight! Oh, my gosh, one of the horsemen stuck a lance right through the body of a warrior! Now the brown men are beginning to whirl something around their heads! Whoa! They hurled rocks or something and two horses went down. They are lying there with the riders' legs trapped under them. I think the horses are dead! This is for real, these guys are killing each other!"

"Quiet!" Sophia said sharply. "I can hear something!"

"Me too. I can hear them shouting ... and scream-ing! Did you see that? One of the soldiers hit a warrior in the neck with a sword! He's down! Wait, another warrior has grabbed him by the shoulders and is pull-ing him out of the way, behind the fight. The wounded man is older, there's gray in his hair, but he's in bad shape. The other guy is kneeling and holding his head off the ground. They seem to be talking to each other. Now the younger one is pulling something off the wounded man's neck; it's a strap with a piece of silver on it. He's putting it around his own neck."

"Oh ... it's gone!" Sophia exclaimed. "Everything's normal again. We just see the houses across the street!"

Both twins turned to stare at the old man, eyes wide.

"What was that all about?" Juan's voice shook. "It wasn't like the movies. Those guys were really killing each other. I'll never forget the screams!"

"Let's go inside," Great Grandfather said. "We need to talk."

CHAPTER 3

Questions

Entering the house, Great Grandfather bustled about the kitchen preparing huevos rancheros. The twins helped, firing non-stop questions.

"How did that happen?" Juan asked, putting out guacamole, sour cream, and salsa.

"Who were those people anyway?" Sophia began heating some flour tortillas.

"That had to be real. They were actually killing each other!" The boy was shaking his head.

"That man had an awful wound in his neck! It was scary!" His sister's voice was low. "Did he die?"

The old man spoke gently. "Hold on, all your questions will be answered. First, let's get breakfast out of the way and then I will fill you in." He shook his head and muttered under his breath to himself, "I can't believe this is happening!"

They sat around a beautiful wooden table, which Great Grandfather had also made by hand, and dived into the meal. The twins knew that it would do no good to ask more questions; he would answer them when he was ready. They never lacked for appetite and breakfast rapidly disappeared. All the while, their relative kept shaking his head and murmuring, "I don't believe it."

Finally, with cups of hot chocolate in front of them, and a steaming cup of coffee for him, Great Grandfather leaned back in his chair and stared at them. "It has finally happened. The medallion is starting to reveal its secret and it seems that you two are the ones to discover it."

"What secret? What is this all about?" Sophia's eyes bored into his.

"Let me start at the beginning." He took a sip of coffee. "It's a long story and time that you hear it in full. You have never been told that our ancestry is Incan."

"I thought the family moved here from Mexico," Juan interrupted.

"It did, around 1620. But, almost 100 years before that, an Incan man made his way out of the Incan Empire, in what is now modern Peru, and settled in the extreme southwest part of Mexico, now the state of Chiapas. If you look on a map, you will find the city of

Tapachula, Mexico. It was near there, close to the Pacific Ocean, that he found a village and settled. Shortly after that, under pressure from Spanish conquistadors, the village moved and relocated in northern Mexico, to the west of what is now the city of Monterrey. In the early years of the 17th century, the grandson of that man moved to the region of Santa Fe, New Mexico. The family became horsemen and prospered for the next 300 years training and trading horses. Finally, Santa Fe became too crowded and my father moved to the San Luis Valley with his horses around 1910."

"You mean that this is the history of our family? We moved here almost 400 years ago!" Juan was astounded. "I thought that your grandfather was the first to come from Mexico about 1875!"

"No, we have a long and proud history in America but it is anchored in the Incan and Aztec Empires. It is time for you to learn that history. It has been passed on to every generation of the family but, because of what you saw this morning, it is particularly important for the two of you."

"Why hasn't anyone told us about this?" Sophia asked.

"That's a good question. The answer is that the one who wears the medallion decides when to pass on the family history. Since I am that person, and you two are the youngest family members, I decided to wait until now before giving you the test of looking through the medallion. For 500 years, the wearer has looked through the silver hole at the rising sun each year on the mornings of the summer and winter solstice. Until now, no one has seen anything."

"Every six months for 500 years?" The twins were incredulous.

"Yes, it's part of the instructions given to the family and carried out ever since."

"You can't be serious. What if someone forgot?"

"No one has because we were ordered to serve the Incan people by the man who was a personal advisor to the Incan Emperor Atahualpa. Pizarro killed the Emperor in 1532. The advisor fled with his young son to the remote city of Pattiti, deep in the mountains. He disguised the approach to the city and it was 10 years before the Spanish stumbled on it. During that time the Incan people looked to him as one of the last leaders in whom they could trust. Not much is known of what he did during those 10 years but any command from him was treated with instant obedience, as though it had come from the Emperor himself!"

"And that advisor was connected to our ancestor?" Sophia was beginning to grasp the sequence of the family history.

"Yes, he was his father."

"But we are in modern times. The Incan Empire was conquered 500 years ago! What could this family in the San Luis Valley of Colorado possibly have to do with a vanished civilization?" Juan was having trouble believing what he was hearing.

"What did you see this morning?" The old man spoke softly.

"Oh. That seemed so real," admitted the boy.

"When the Spanish finally found Pattiti, they attacked immediately. Part of that battle is what you saw through the medallion. The man you saw dying was Qist, advisor to Emperor Atahualpa. The warrior holding him was his son Adzul, the father of our family. As he died, Qist gave Adzul the medallion, along with directions about it and about two Incan traditions that the family was to follow. I will explain both of them to you."

"Will you teach us the family history?" Sophia inquired.

"It is a long story," replied Great Grandfather, "which I will begin this morning. Let's go out on the front porch."

CHAPTER 4
Flight

ADZUL SPRINTED UP A STREET, quickly wrapping the sling around his waist as he ran. He had seen the captain yell and point after he had deliberately mocked him with a smile. Even though he didn't understand their language, he knew that the Spaniards would be coming after him. They were a cruel people; during the last 20 years of war, there were countless reports of their horrible tortures. It was no longer a time to fight. Aside from the vow to his father, the insult meant the worst possible fate if he were captured. At the very least, he would be slowly skinned alive in front of the captain. The mountains were his only hope; he had to make good his escape.

As he ran, he took stock of his situation. It was midafternoon and already getting cold. When night fell, the temperature would drop below freezing. When the enemy had unexpectedly appeared, all the men had shed their heavy wool tunics, hats, and robes to fight. They had only worn their light armor shirts. This cloth, created with a special weave known only to the people of Pattiti, replaced the bulkier armor worn throughout the rest of the Empire. It could withstand the direct slash of a sword, or the thrust of a lance, but it was quite thin and provided little protection from the bitter cold of the high mountains.

He was debating whether to duck into one of the doorways to seek clothing when shouts sounded behind. Glancing back, Adzul was startled to see horsemen rounding a corner waving swords in the air. He hadn't expected them so soon. Little did he know of the reward which the captain had offered, riches that caused men to ignore the fighting and spur their horses through the Incan lines. Seven had broken free and were in hot pursuit; there was no time to do anything but run.

He knew he could not outpace the horses, so he decided to use narrow streets and alleys that twisted through the city. Realizing the soldiers could go straight out the main thoroughfare and trap him on the outskirts, he deliberately slowed down. The riders quickly gained on him and went into a frenzy of spurring their mounts to be the first to reach him.

When they were within yards, he suddenly cut right and sprinted down a small side street. The strategy worked perfectly!

With no officer to think for them, the men believed their quarry was tiring and poured into the street after him. But Adzul was not close to being tired. At 5'6," his body was lean and tough and used to long runs at high altitude. His wide-set eyes, above the prominent Incan nose, showed keen intelligence. Shoulder-length black hair was held in place by a red headband; his only ornaments were gold plugs inserted in the bottom of each earlobe. Although he was the son of an Incan nobleman, he had trained from adolescence to be a warrior and to lead warriors. He had swum in icy rivers, gone for days without food, spent nights without clothing; he was well suited for the ordeal ahead.

Running easily, he zigzagged his way through the city. Although he tried to lose the horsemen they managed to stay close behind, cleverly forming a line so no one was crowded out as they thundered down narrow alleys. Luck smiled on him though because the lead horse slipped on the pavement in a tight corner and went down. The rest of the group barely avoided a massive pileup, but it took several minutes for the rider to get his horse on its feet and moving, while the other Spaniards yelled and cursed the delay. Adzul gained precious moments for the race that he knew was coming at the edge of the city.

Reaching the outskirts, the warrior made a right turn and sprinted for the bottom of the staircase road ahead. It was his escape route and climbed straight up a high ridge, bordering the city on the north. Characteristic of all Incan roads, it was literally a stone staircase ascending the mountain. Since the Incan beast of burden was the llama, easily able to handle a stairway, the roads simply went up and down the terrain. The conquistador horses, however, were at a decided disadvantage because footing was slippery on the smooth rock and the steepness slowed them to a lunging walk.

The bottom of the looming ridge, almost a mile high, was only 200 yards away but the riders appeared before he had covered half the distance. Adzul reached the lowest stair barely ahead of the first horseman and began racing up in great leaps. The horse balked at the unfamiliar footing so the rider quickly moved it onto the dirt beside the stairs, lashing and spurring it mercilessly, but the slope was so steep that Adzul began to pull away.

One of the other riders rushed up and leveled a blunderbuss at the fleeing man. There was a loud boom and a sheet of flame poured out of the trumpet-like end of the barrel. The warrior above suddenly fell, grabbing his left thigh. The conquistadors jumped off their horses, whooping and hollering, certain that they had their man. A couple of them even started up the stairs on foot to capture him. But suddenly he was on the move again, although climbing more slowly. There was a scramble as the soldiers remounted and began forcing their mounts up the slippery stairs, with cruel spurs bloodying the animals' sides. The ridge was so steep that the men who tried to climb their horses on the dirt to the side were actually slower than those on the road.

The blunderbuss, normally totally unreliable at any range, had raked the outside of Adzul's thigh with a piece of shrapnel, leaving a wound 8-inches long and ½ an inch deep. He had been totally stunned, at first believing one of the riders had caught up and slashed him with a sword. When he grabbed the leg and fell, all the men were still at the bottom of the hill; he couldn't figure out how they had attacked him. The Incan thought the guns were primarily for scaring people because they rarely hit anyone. Seeing that the gash was not serious, although extremely painful and bleeding freely, he resumed the climb.

The warrior's objective was a flattened area about halfway to the top of the ridge. On it, close to the edge, were positioned several round boulders almost 8-feet tall and weighing nearly a ton. From below, they were almost impossible to see because of the steep angle of the slope. It had taken many men using thick ropes to get them in place but they represented one method, learned through years of fighting, to neutralize the tactical advantage of the conquistadors' horses.

Adzul forced pain from his mind and focused on the flat area hundreds of yards above. He willed himself to run as before and, although the leg became streaked with blood, soon regained his pace. Quick glances back showed that he was increasing his lead and he estimated he would reach the flat area before the soldiers were half way. He continued up two stairs at a time, still breathing easily in spite of the exertion. The sun had slid almost to the huge peaks rising on his left when he reached the small terrace with the boulders. It was roughly 30-yards wide, with the stone road crossing it to where the stairs resumed.

One of the boulders was just to his right, 20 feet from the edge of the slope. A stone wedge, inserted at its base, prevented it from moving. On the ground was a hefty wooden mallet. Adzul grabbed it and slammed the head against the wedge, knocking it clear. Racing around to the other side of the boulder, he braced his back against it and began to push with all the strength in his legs.

CHAPTER 5
Boulders

IN SPITE OF THE lowering temperatures, sweat popped out on the warrior's forehead as he strained against the rock. Normally, it took two men to move it. It didn't budge and he redoubled his efforts, straining with all his might and ignoring the screaming pain from his wound. The muscles in his thighs and calves were bulging like cords and his breath came in gasps. He could hear shouts below as the Spaniards drove their horses up the steep steps. Crouching even lower he exerted every bit of power that he had, groaning with the effort. The great rock suddenly gave a slight move and tipped forward. With a mighty heave, Adzul started it rolling toward the edge of the stairs. When the boulder nosed over the top step, gravity took hold and it plunged down the stairs gaining momentum at every bounce. Soon it was hurtling down the road!

The soldiers, focused on trying to force their horses to climb faster, glanced up to see the enormous rock bearing down on them. Shouting in alarm, they leaped off and dragged the animals to the safety of the grass beside the road. Just above them the boulder hit the edge of a step and bounded into the air, passing completely above their heads! They all turned to watch it speed down the mountain. Raising their fists in triumph they swung around to look up the hill, jeering at the Incan. *sent down 3 boulders in a row*

But Adzul had wasted no time to see the result of his effort. Racing to a smaller boulder, he had smashed the wedge loose and launched it almost immediately. This rock was positioned slightly to the left of the stairs and came silently down the grassy slope like a freight train. The two soldiers who had taken refuge to that side of the road never had a chance. It struck them full on as they turned to look uphill, killing both instantly. Their horses, sensing the danger, had pulled away and stampeded wildly across the slope. For a second there was stunned silence among the Spaniards, then shouts of alarm as a third boulder was launched down the right side of the stairs!

The conquistadors scattered out across the steep hillside to escape the oncoming rock, barely able to keep upright and hang on to their frightened horses. By the time they had brought the animals under control and made their way back to the road, Adzul was halfway to the summit. To let him escape meant almost certain death at the hands of the captain. They redoubled their efforts to get up the stairs, whipping the horses with quirts. *– riding whip w/short handle*

Upon reaching the summit, Adzul looked back down the slope. The riders were crossing the terrace where the boulders had been positioned. The road crossed the top of the ridge and descended in stairs for almost a mile to a narrow valley below that snaked northward. Knowing that the riders would come downhill rapidly on the grass, he started down the stairs in great leaps of four to five steps at a time, arms flung out to either side for balance and black hair streaming behind his head. Miraculously reaching the bottom without a fall, he heard faint whoops and yells as the Spaniards crossed the top and began charging down the slope. They would reach the bottom in minutes. He ran for his life.

The sun had dropped behind massive snowcapped peaks to the west and the valley was already deep in shadow. He could feel the temperature dropping and knew that night was not far off. The dark would bring invisibility. The Spaniards understood this also and would push their horses to the limit coming down the ridge. He willed himself to run at top speed in spite of the pain and stiffening in his wounded leg.

The road ahead curved to the right and soon blocked his view of the riders. As he ran, he searched the hills to either side for any place of concealment. To the left, snowbanks came down almost to the valley floor. To the right, steep grassy slopes mounted a high ridge. Not a tree or bush grew in the rugged terrain.

In minutes he would be caught in the open against five armed and mounted soldiers. The outcome was certain. Being captured alive was out of the question, so he would fight to the death. For the first time in his life he didn't want the protection of armor against the thrust of a lance or sword, and he was just beginning to pull the shirt off when he saw the rock.

About 100 yards up the hill to the right was a medium-sized boulder in the grass. It looked just big enough to hide him. He stopped and dropped to the road, putting his ear to the smooth rock. There was no vibration from the horses' hooves, which meant that the riders were still on the ridge. There might be enough time. Springing to his feet, he began scrambling up the steep slope. It seemed incredibly slow because his sandals kept slipping and the dry grass he grabbed pulled right out of the dirt.

He was a little more than halfway to the rock when he heard the faint thunder of hooves echoing off the valley walls. In minutes, they would come around the bend and he would be totally exposed. Putting every ounce of strength into arms and legs, he scrambled up the last 40 yards on all fours like a dog and collapsed in a ball behind the rock, just as the five Spaniards came around the corner! Intent on catching the fleeing warrior, they passed below at a dead run with their eyes focused on the curving road ahead.

Adzul knew they would be back as soon as the road straightened and they could see that he was no longer ahead of them. The boulder on the hillside was too obvious; they would spot it immediately. Still gasping from the climb, he sprang up and began to move further uphill in the lowering darkness. He had only gained 30 yards when he heard the pounding hooves that signaled the returning horses. Dropping flat in the low grass, he spread arms and legs wide apart to present as small a profile as possible. He knew that he would be hard to spot in the dusk.

Sure enough, the soldiers saw the boulder and immediately reined in their horses. He could hear them talking excitedly. Lifting his head slightly to take a peek, he saw two of them dismount and begin climbing the slope, swords in hand. Hampered by heavy armor, their progress was slow and it was almost completely dark by the time they reached the rock. Even so the marks of his body were clearly visible in the grass, and they began shouting down to their companions and pointing up the hill. More shouting ensued as the soldiers on the road exhorted them to keep going. After a hurried conversation, the two men spread out and started towards his position. They called to each other constantly as they slowly drew near.

The warrior was almost certain the approaching men couldn't see him, but the distance between them was rapidly shrinking. At close range, their swords would be extremely dangerous in the dark. Rising to his feet, he unwrapped the sling and loaded it with a rock from the pouch at his belt. The sound of the 5-foot straps whirling in the air was unmistakable and shouts of alarm rang out from the two soldiers.

Adzul fired at the voice of the man to his left. He aimed low because he knew the conquistador was on hands and knees. Years of experience gave him unerring accuracy and the rock flew true. There was a thud and a loud scream, followed by the sound of a body rolling down the hill accompanied by more screaming. The rock had hit the man just outside the breastplate of the armor, shattering his left shoulder. Unable to control himself on the steep terrain he rolled all the way to the road, shrieking with every impact of his shoulder on the hard dirt.

The sling was already whirling again before the wounded soldier had covered 10 yards. The man on the right, realizing the danger, stopped shouting and scuttled back towards the safety of the boulder, trying to be as quiet as possible. A rock whizzing past his head convinced him to follow his companion down to the road!

By now the soldiers below had built a small fire against the chilling cold. At an altitude of 10,000 feet, the temperature would fall well below freezing before dawn. In the flickering light, Adzul could see them tending to the wounded man. Within a few minutes, the second man rejoined them and there was much talking and pointing up the hill. When no one left the fire, he knew that he was safe for the rest of the night. None of the Spaniards wanted to face his sling in the dark.

Silently, he traversed the hillside until he was a quarter of a mile beyond the conquistadors and could no longer see the fire. Edging his way down to the road, he took time to bind the wound on his thigh with strips cut from his loincloth. As he worked, he realized that the medallion was no longer hot on his skin. When the leg was bandaged he set off at a trot that ate up the miles, millions of stars in the clear sky lighting his way.

CHAPTER 6
Slings

GREAT GRANDFATHER stopped talking, eyes still closed visualizing the scene. Almost an hour had passed, but it seemed like minutes to the twins.

His eyes popped open. "That's all for now. I've got work to do in the garden."

"But, you just got started!" Sophia was totally caught up in the story and didn't want it to end.

The old man grinned. "It's a long story and we'll have plenty of time for it this summer and fall. Besides, if I told it at one sitting, you two would be fast asleep long before I finished!"

"No way!" Juan protested.

"It's that long?" Sophia asked.

"The medallion was involved with every generation of our family for 500 years. That's a lot of history! But you have other things to learn as well." He got up and disappeared into the house, returning with a small wooden box. From it he took what looked like two balls of leather string.

"What in the world is this?" Juan asked as he was handed one of the balls.

"Stand up and shake it out," Great Grandfather directed, handing the second ball to Sophia.

When they did, the twins found they were holding two thin leather straps attached to either side of a round piece of leather 6 inches wide. They had to lift their hands almost above their heads for the leather patches not to drag on the floor. They stared at Great Grandfather.

"You are holding Incan slings." His eyes were steady. "It was their most effective weapon!"

Juan's eyes widened. "How does it work?"

The old man took the leather strings from Sofia and hopped off the porch. Reaching into a small sack at his belt, he pulled out a stone the size of an egg. He placed the stone in the round piece of leather attached to the strings and lowered it to just above the ground. Stepping clear of the porch, he suddenly started swinging the strings around his head. The rock was held securely in the pouch by centrifugal force. Faster and faster he swung until the strings were a blur. Suddenly the rock flew out of the pouch like a bullet, burying itself in a tree trunk on the other side of the street!

The kids' mouths fell open and they stared at the old man.

"Wow, that's totally cool!" Juan could hardly believe what he had seen.

"I want to learn how to do that!" Sophia was beside herself with excitement.

They ran across the street and found that the stone was deeply embedded in the tree. Juan had to use his pocketknife to pry it out! Returning to the house, he handed the rock to Great Grandfather.

"That's got to be 35 yards away!" As starting quarterback for the middle school team, Juan was used to calculating distances. "How did you do that?"

"My father taught me when I was younger than you. His grandfather taught him, as he was taught by his grandfather, and so on back through the family history. Every generation has learned the sling; it was part of the instructions from Qist to Adzul."

"It's so powerful! I had to dig the rock out with my knife!"

"Yes. With full velocity, the rock leaves the sling at around 100 miles per hour. The Incan fighters could kill a horse by hitting the animal in the head! At close range, it would shatter the skull of a man. They used other weapons, but the sling was the most deadly. It was utilized throughout the ancient world. The Bible speaks of David killing Goliath with a stone thrown from a sling. It also speaks of men who were so accurate with it that they could split a hair at 20 yards!"

"Is it hard to learn?" Sophia was examining the straps.

"No, but precise accuracy takes a lot of work. I would suggest that you practice every day at one of the empty fields outside town. You need to stay well away from houses because the chances are good that you will break a window, or hit someone, before you learn control. Also, keep well away from each other when you practice because in the beginning the rocks will fly in all directions, and you don't want to hurt one another. Finally, please be discreet with your friends; this is not a skill that we teach outside the family."

The twins nodded their agreement.

Great Grandfather went on. "When you can hit a can five times in a row at 30 yards, come back and show me. Then I'll have something else for you."

"Something else? But what about the story?" In spite of his desire to learn the sling, Juan wanted to hear more of Adzul's escape.

"We're all busy during the week. You have your summer jobs and I have customers for the garden. Come back next Saturday morning at 8:00 and we'll continue."

On their way home, Juan and Sophia decided to practice for an hour every day. The next morning they were on their bikes at 5:30, headed to an abandoned field outside of town.

CHAPTER 7
Pursuit

THE TEMPERATURE DROPPED well below freezing and bit at every part of Adzul's exposed skin. The sleeveless armor shirt gave some protection to his upper body, but exertion was his only defense against the cold. Properly dressed, he would have been wearing a warm sleeveless wool tunic reaching almost to his knees. It was called an uncu. A long wool cloak, called a yacolla, would be wrapped around him over the uncu, and a thick wool cap with earflaps would have completed his wardrobe. Without the luxury of such clothes, he willed himself to ignore the frigid air and concentrate on putting miles between him and the soldiers. Dawn found him reduced to a slow trot, doggedly moving ahead with hunger and thirst knotting his stomach.

Entering a wider valley, the road approached a flat, grassy area with a stream running through it. Intent on slaking a raging thirst, it took Adzul a minute to realize there were llamas lying beside the stream and two men squatting by a small fire. Spotting a pile of packs near the animals, he knew they were traders headed south to Pattiti. He gave a low whistle as he approached so as not to alarm them.

The two men stood to greet him, noting his armor shirt and wound. Without hesitation they offered him food, water, and fresh cloth to bandage his leg. As they watched, he wolfed down strips of dried meat, small boiled potatoes, and cocoa leaves. Between mouthfuls, he described the events of the past 24 hours.

"So, they finally found Pattiti." The older one frowned. "We've brought goods from far to the north to trade in the city."

Adzul knew men like these were gone for months at a time, trading in lands far beyond the borders of the Incan Empire, and out of touch with current events. "Approach the city with care," he warned. "I don't know how the battle turned out."

Both men expressed sorrow at the death of Qist. They knew of his inspiration and leadership during the long years of fighting after the Emperor was murdered.

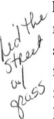

(handwritten margin note: lid the street w/ grass)

"Your father was responsible for keeping the city hidden from the invaders for many years." The younger man smiled. "He disguised the only road from the south by having the pavement torn out for 15 miles from Pattiti to the next small town. The ground was replanted with grass and strewn with rock. It still looks totally undisturbed. This northern road also disappears. It is only used by traders and is so remote that it has never been discovered."

"My father did all that while I was still a child," Adzul explained.

"He was a wise man and the Incan people owe him much. Let us supply you with food and clothing. The horsemen will be coming soon." The men turned to their packs and pulled out sandals, woolen tunic, cloak, and cap. Adzul put on the tunic and hat and fashioned the cloak into a pack to sling across his back. In it he put the meat, frozen potatoes, and cocoa leaves that they pressed on him.

"Be wary of the soldiers," he cautioned. "I think there are only four now because of the man I wounded last night. They are dangerous."

The older trader grinned. "We will take to the high slopes, but they are not looking for llamas. It is you they seek."

"If it were not for my father's orders, I would ambush them and take my chances," replied the warrior grimly. Enormously refreshed by the food and water, he thanked the traders and started off as they began packing the llamas. When he looked back an hour later, they were mere specks high on the valley walls.

Adzul covered many miles that day. He didn't see the Spanish riders until early afternoon when he crossed a high ridge. They were far back in the valley that he had just left. The distance was so great that he doubted they could see him, but he marveled at their persistence. They had to be out of food and yet they kept coming. He had no way of knowing the fear that drove them.

The road followed a series of valleys winding north, surrounded by enormous mountains. Running well into each night to offset the greater speed of the horses, Adzul managed to keep ahead of the riders for the next few days, encountering a few small villages along the way. As he reached each one he stopped briefly to acquire potatoes and dried meat, alerting the villagers to his pursuers. He urged them to flee into the nearby mountains until the danger had passed and to leave no food for the Spaniards to steal.

Despite the warrior's superb conditioning, the pace began to take its toll on his body. Dark circles and hollows appeared under his eyes. The little body fat that he possessed disappeared, giving him an emaciated look. After two days the paved road ceased, to be replaced by a simple path through the grass, and he wondered if that was due to his father's strategy long ago. He knew the pursuers had to check the occasional side valley, in case he had gone into hiding, but he dared not slow the pace. He was beginning to be desperately tired and knew that he could not hold out much longer.

Eight days after leaving Pattiti, Adzul realized he was nearing the northern border of the Empire. The dim track that he followed would soon give way to a trader's path through the northern mountains, clearly marked by stone cairns. He remembered hearing that the first 50 miles followed one narrow valley, almost a canyon, out of which there was no possibility of climbing due to impossibly steep walls. With no place for him to hide, the trailing horsemen would have the advantage in speed and would simply run him down. He had to do something.

A solution presented itself as he ran under a leaden sky one morning. The path entered a valley that curved away to his left. To his right was a hill, above which he could see the slopes of another valley that seemed to bear east. He instantly decided to take a chance on unknown ground.

As he carefully climbed the hill, stepping only on rocks to leave no trace of his passing, light snow began to fall. When he crossed the top, he judged the riders were still at least two hours behind him. He rushed down the far slope, trying to cover as much ground as possible before the falling snow revealed his tracks.

CHAPTER 8

Practice

GREAT GRANDFATHER glanced at his watch. A week had passed, and the three had gathered again on his porch in the early morning sun. "That's all we have time for today. Do you have plans for next Saturday morning?"

The twins shook their heads, disappointment in their eyes that the story had ended.

"How's it going with the slings?" he asked, changing the subject.

Juan and Sophia looked at each other and giggled.

"Well," she began, "it's a good thing you told us to spread out!"

"Although we may be more of a danger to ourselves than each other," Juan interjected, pulling up a pant leg to reveal a big black and blue mark on the top of his foot. "I almost couldn't walk for a day after doing this!"

"I haven't hit myself yet," Sophia said grinning. "But I have thrown the whole sling out into the field several times, when I let go of both straps by mistake!"

The old man chuckled. "Nothing the rest of the family hasn't done over the past 500 years!"

Indeed, the kids had found the ancient weapon tricky to master. There was the problem of starting the swing quickly enough so the rock didn't fall out of the pouch. Next was learning when to let go of one leather string. That first week, rocks were flying everywhere: straight up into the air, or straight down into the ground, or onto one's foot (as Juan had experienced)! Sometimes the missile would shoot off to the right or left, even straight back — everywhere but the direction they wanted it to go!

In fact, Juan had also released the two strings at once and seen the entire apparatus fly into the field. He solved this problem by tying a slipknot in the end of one string and slipping it over his index finger so it was attached to his hand like a yoyo. In some inexplicable way, on at least one occasion the sling had wound up wrapped around their necks! By unspoken agreement, neither of them mentioned it to their mentor.

Their enthusiasm was unchecked, however, because they could see the tremendous force the sling generated and they understood that it was just a matter of time until they mastered it. They were awed by the idea that ancient throwers could split a hair or snap a steel sword blade.

As they left, Great Grandfather gave them a hint. "You might try following through with your arm in the direction that you want the rock to go."

On the way home, Juan commented, "That makes total sense. When I throw a football, my throwing arm should wind up pointed at the receiver."

Sophia, who was an outstanding volleyball player, agreed. "When I'm setting up someone for a slam, I always follow through with my hands in the direction that I sent the ball."

The next morning she made a breakthrough. Releasing the strap as it flew past her right ear and thrusting her right arm forward after the release, caused the rock to fly out in front of her. As she practiced this move, the stone began to fly consistently in front of her rather than to the sides or behind. The angle of flight was erratic, sometimes too high and other times too low, but she had made significant progress. After sharing her discovery with Juan, they both improved rapidly. By midweek they had learned to lower the trajectory, and their rocks were beginning to kick up dirt around the Coke cans. On Friday morning they each scored a direct hit! The loud 'clank,' plus significant dents in the cans, filled them with excitement.

"I can't wait to tell Great Grandfather!" exclaimed Juan.

"I'll bet he never thought we could do it this fast!" Sophia chimed in.

When they assembled on his porch the next day, Great Grandfather listened to their report with a big smile. "Good job! I knew you would figure it out! All your athletics have really helped!"

"You should have heard it!" Juan crowed. "That can must have jumped a foot! We're going to hit five out of five in no time flat!"

"Great! How far was the can?"

"Oh, about from here to that rosebush." The boy pointed to a flowering rose 25 feet away.

"Excellent!" The old man grinned and pointed to the tree across the street where his stone had embedded. "Keep in mind the objective is 30 yards, not 30 feet."

There was dead silence.

"Oh, I forgot. That's a bit different," Sophia spoke softly. "I think we've gotten a little carried away with our success."

"Not at all," Great Grandfather assured her. "The sling is difficult to master, especially at distance. You both have done amazingly well for only 10 hours of practice. Keep up the good work!" He leaned back in the rocker, eyes gazing up into the blue sky. "Now, where was I?"

CHAPTER 9
The River

Adzul was relieved to see the valley was not a dead end but continued more or less straight east after bending away from the track. The snow stopped in midafternoon and a cold sun broke through the clouds. Winter was not far off and would fill every valley with deep snow, making travel impossible. He had to get out of the high mountains soon or he would be faced with a second threat to survival. Having abandoned the security of the well-marked trader's path, he was faced with having to negotiate unknown terrain. He thought about hiding for a few days and returning to the marked trail, but the uncertainty of eluding the Spaniards convinced him to keep going. He knew somewhere to the east the mountains ended, but he had no idea how far away that was.

The cloak and tunic kept his body warm, but the sandals offered little protection from the snow and his feet became red with cold. Food was becoming a problem. He had only a few potatoes and a handful of maize left from the last village, and there would be no people living in this remote valley. Chinchillas could be hunted, but that took time and he wanted to put as much distance as possible between himself and the road. Water was available from many small springs that flowed down the mountainsides, so he pressed steadily on.

As the days passed and there was no sign of pursuit, the warrior began to feel he had at last escaped the conquistadors. The valley wound steadily to the east between gigantic slopes that swept up to snow-covered peaks. Huge boulders were scattered across the brown grass that covered the ground, the result of constant avalanches roaring down the mountains during winter. Nothing moved in the vast stillness of the Andes except the occasional speck of a condor riding the air currents high above. He was alone.

One afternoon, five days after leaving the road, he was bending to drink from a stream when movement caught his eye in a nearby pile of rocks. He had finished the last potato two days before and hunger was gnawing at his belly. Unwrapping the sling from his waist, he loaded it and slipped behind a boulder so only his eyes peeked out. Shortly, a small gray animal about 6 inches tall popped up on the rock pile and stood on its hind legs staring in his direction. For long minutes it remained motionless. Finally, satisfied there was no threat, it jumped to the ground and started busily nosing around the grass. The whir of the sling caused it to stand up again and stare, but it was too late. The speeding rock killed it instantly.

Without retrieving the body, Adzul reloaded the sling and waited. Chinchillas live in colonies and he knew others would appear. An hour later, eight little bodies were lying beside a small fire of twigs from nearby bushes. There was little meat on them, but the man was almost starving and he left only the bones. Although it was not enough to fill his stomach, he was energized and set off at good pace. If he had had the luxury of two extra days, he would have made chinchilla moccasins but he didn't dare take the time. The next morning he discovered another colony, but feeling the pressure to move on he stayed only long enough to kill a few.

A week after leaving the road, Adzul came to a river rushing across the valley. It sprang from a glacier almost a mile above him to the left and disappeared into a narrow canyon to his right and was far too deep and swift to cross. He would have to climb up to the glacier and ford where the water was shallow. Since it was late afternoon, he decided to wait until morning to make the ascent. Turning to the right, he walked among boulders lining the bank. Two hundred yards downstream, with a roar the water cascaded over the edge of a sheer cliff! At least 120 feet below was a large pool into which the waterfall plunged and was sucked immediately into steep rapids churning and foaming down the mountain. Clouds of mist rose from the falls, soaking sheer rock cliffs to either side. There was no way down.

The mighty waterfall suddenly became insignificant because of the panorama that met his shocked eyes! Beyond the cliff there were no gray mountains stretching up to snowcapped peaks! There was only empty space extending endlessly until sky met earth far in the distance. Below him, miles away, a vast emerald green carpet stretched in every direction. He could hardly believe it. He had reached the eastern edge of the great mountains! The land at the foot of the mountains offered food, shelter, and escape from the winter storms. A wave of relief swept over him; the ordeal of his flight from Pattiti was over! Tomorrow he would find a way around the cliffs.

Picking his way back upstream, Adzul headed for a pile of rocks he had noticed on the other side of the valley. He was sure he would find a chinchilla colony there and he was desperately hungry. Hiding behind a boulder he loaded the sling and waited, eyes riveted on the rocks. Sure enough, after awhile there was a flicker of gray and one of the little animals appeared. Patience and skill over the next 90 minutes rewarded him with enough rodents for a small meal.

As night fell, he sat with his back against a large boulder and watched the embers dying in his tiny fire. With the edge taken off his hunger and the prospect of escaping the mountains before winter, he was filled with energy and enthusiasm. Somehow he would solve the problem of the cliffs. When the fire went out he lay against the rock and pulled the flaps of his cap over his ears, hiked his legs up under the warmth of the cloak, and drifted asleep to the comforting sound of the river.

CHAPTER 10
Captured!

In the pre-dawn gray, Adzul's eyes flew open. He lay completely still, uncertain what had roused him. Tattered pieces of fog were blowing through the boulder field and mist was rising off the river. With a start, he realized the medallion was warm against his chest and getting hotter by the second! Simultaneously, the hair on the back of his neck stood up and his arms felt prickly; both were signs of danger that he had experienced in war. He studied everything within his range of vision. Nothing moved. Knowing he was almost invisible in the dim light, he shifted his head slightly to get a better view of the river above and below him.

For long minutes there was no visible sign of trouble, but the heat of the medallion told him otherwise. Suddenly a flicker of movement 80 feet away at the edge of the river caught his attention. Where there had been nothing seconds before, he now saw the outline of a crouched man with a sword in hand and the bulk of armor on his chest. It was a Spanish soldier! How had they found him?

Minutes dragged by and the fog grew thicker, almost hiding the figure. All at once the Spaniard stood up and stepped away from the bank to disappear among the boulders. He was apparently satisfied that the warrior was not in the vicinity.

A faint clink not more than 20 feet away alerted Adzul to the presence of another soldier. Just beyond his head he saw legs walk to the water and stop. He remained absolutely motionless, knowing the man was looking for him up and down the bank. If he were spotted, he would have no chance to defend himself. Fortunately, it was still dark enough that his gray wool cloak and hat blended perfectly into the slight overhang of the boulder above him. After what seemed an eternity there was a muttered curse and the man strode away, passing within 6 feet of his head!

Adzul lay still until the clinking faded. Although the medallion was still burning, he guessed he was safe for the moment because the soldiers would spread to search other areas along the bank. They knew they had him trapped against the swift, deep river. But the valley was 300 yards wide, and there were plenty of places to hide among the boulders. Easing himself to an upright position, he loaded the sling and stepped away from the rock. Instantly, something loomed up behind him. A sixth sense warned him and he started to whirl around, but it was too late. A heavy blow from the handle of a sword drove him to his knees. As he tried to rise, more blows rained down on his head and shoulders, accompanied by curses in Spanish, until he was stretched out unconscious. His attacker yelled to the others and they came running, one with his sword raised to deliver a killing thrust.

"Stop!" the leader cried. "The captain wants him alive. He promised gold for bringing him back. You know how he delights in cutting out their tongues and eyes; he prolongs their agony for days while slowly skinning them alive and then putting the body on a bed of coals. This vermin will beg for death before it is over!"

The conquistadors had to satisfy themselves by kicking Adzul's limp body repeatedly before tying him up.

When he woke, Adzul found himself cruelly bound. There was a rope around his neck nearly strangling him. It was tied to his bound wrists and from them around both knees. The whole apparatus had been drawn so tightly that he was pulled into a fetal position, unable to move. His cloak and hat had been stripped off. In the dark, the men had not seen the armor shirt under his tunic. It had almost certainly saved him from broken ribs, but every part of his body hurt from the stomping he had received.

The sun was well up by now but the soldiers were sleeping, sprawled on the ground around him. The Spaniards had reached the river at midnight and immediately started searching for their prey. He was so disguised by the cloak that they hadn't spotted him until he stood up hours later. Now that Adzul was securely in their possession, they had given in to an exhausted sleep.

An hour later one of the men stirred. He raised his head to stare at the warrior and then stood up and walked to where Adzul lay. Studying the ropes to make sure they hadn't loosened, he noticed the leather strap around the warrior's neck.

"What's this?" he muttered to himself, yanking on the leather. When the medallion appeared from under Adzul's tunic, the soldier sucked in his breath and glanced quickly around to see if anyone else was awake. "A little bonus for me in case the captain forgets his promise of gold," he whispered softly to himself. He yanked on the strap, but it didn't come free. "I'll just cut you loose," he muttered, reaching for a knife and grabbing the medallion.

As the Spaniard's hand closed over the piece of silver, a look of shock filled his face and he groaned through clenched teeth. The metal was literally burning through the skin of his hand! He dared not cry out because he knew the others would kill him for trying to steal something for himself. He shook his hand violently, but the silver wouldn't part from the charred palm. He finally grabbed the thong with his free hand and ripped the silver from his smoking flesh. He staggered to the bank of the river and dropping to his knees, plunged the burned hand under water.

When the medallion came free, it fell directly on the rope connecting Adzul's neck and wrists. Instantly, it burned through the fibers and dropped to his chest. Straining his wrists, he managed to touch the rope binding them to the surface of the medallion. The rope was immediately burned through. It took only a moment to slip the medallion from around his neck and apply the silver to the rope still tied around his legs. Part of his mind registered that the metal, while hot enough to sear through rope, had no effect on his fingers. In seconds he was free!

Adzul stood up and replaced the medallion around his neck, tucking it under the armor shirt. He bent to scoop his sling from the dirt beside him. At the movement, the wounded conquistador by the river turned and saw that he was free. Grabbing his sword, in spite of the pain it caused, he leaped up and screamed to the other men. As they all jumped up, the warrior knew there was no time to run. He took three quick steps and leaped into the rushing river!

The shock of the icy water took his breath away. In the few seconds before he went over the falls, he wrapped the sling around his right hand and gripped it tightly. It was the one thing he didn't want to lose if he survived the fall. Then he was swept over the lip and plummeted down, flailing and windmilling his arms. He knew he must not land on his side or head because from such a height the surface of the water would be like rock and could shatter skull or bones. At the last instant, he managed to get his body upright and hit the pool feet first with an enormous splash.

The pool was deep and he shot down under the pressure of tons of water. No stranger to swimming, he began kicking and stroking toward the left bank as soon as his momentum slowed. From above, he had seen the current in the pool and did not want to be pulled into the rapids. When his head broke the surface, he was 10 yards from the bank and almost at the end of the pool. The current was rapidly dragging him towards the drop-off. He kicked with all his strength, but his left foot didn't seem to work properly and gave him no thrust. He lunged forward with great splashing strokes, but the distance was too great.

As the roar of the rapids filled his ears, he realized he had failed his father because he knew he wouldn't survive the rocks below. But, 3 feet from the boiling rapids his right foot slammed into something. It was a large boulder sticking up from the bottom of the pool. As his leg was swept across its top, he somehow got one foot under his body and gave a mighty push. It propelled him half out of the water in a desperate dive toward the bank. His outstretched hands slid across slippery rocks, finally closing in a death grip on the jagged edge of one that had split apart. The force of the current was so great that it swung the rest of his body around until he was parallel to the shore in shallower water.

Gasping for breath, Adzul managed to get to his feet and stagger away from the river. His left ankle would barely support him and he collapsed on a patch of dirt, sprawled on his back. Gasping for breath, he knew he was lucky to be alive. If it hadn't been for the underwater boulder, he wouldn't have made it. Movement above caught his attention; four heads were peering down from the edge of the waterfall.

Outraged that the captive had escaped their clutches, the conquistadors screamed curses at him and shook their fists. There was no way down the cliffs and they faced the grim prospect of returning to their captain empty-handed. Adzul could see their mouths moving, but no sound reached him over the roar of the water. He raised his right fist weakly in the air, grinning at them in triumph, and passed out.

CHAPTER 11
The Empire

THE KIDS WAITED UNTIL Great Grandfather ended the story before peppering him with questions. There was something about the way he talked, with eyes closed as though he was actually seeing the events, that kept them from interrupting. Sophia had started to bring a pencil and paper to jot quick notes during the tale. Each episode raised points that needed clarification and this morning was no exception.

"Was there really a trail for traders that went north from South America?" she asked.

"Farther than that," he replied. "It undoubtedly extended all the way through Central America and into what is now Mexico. In fact, it probably connected to a number of trails that stretched across North America."

"How do you know?"

"Well, I don't know specifically but evidence shows there was extensive commerce throughout the Northern and Southern Hemispheres before the Europeans arrived."

"Evidence?" She raised her eyebrows.

"Yes. In their digs, archeologists are continually finding artifacts that originated elsewhere. For example, shells from the Pacific Northwest showed up in a Plains Indian excavation in Nebraska, and pottery shards from the Southwest appeared in the ruins of an Iroquois fort near the Great Lakes. Incan trinkets were found in ancient California settlements. Previously, historians thought only primitive peoples sparsely settled the Americas. Modern research seems to indicate there were large, sophisticated populations interacting with each other throughout the two continents."

"What about these roads that Qist allegedly tore up?" Juan was always interested in military strategy.

"The Incans were incredible stonemasons. At the height of the Empire, they had about 25,000 miles of paved roads throughout their territory. They were made of smoothed rocks, perfectly fitted together. Check online about the buildings at Machu Pichu. They were made from stone blocks matched so skillfully no mortar was needed to hold them in place."

"I bet Qist's men had a heck of a time tearing up 20 miles of those roads," Juan mused.

"It wasn't only their stonework that was sophisticated," Great Grandfather went on. "They had methods of refining gold that the Europeans hadn't developed. Gold wasn't meaningful to them as money or riches; it was a sign of importance. Did you see anything unusual about the buildings you observed through the medallion?"

The twins thought for a minute before Sophia exclaimed, "Yes, one of them seemed to be very bright!"

"I think I remember that," her brother said, "but I was really focused on the fighting."

The old man nodded. "The building you saw was probably covered with a thin sheet of gold." At their astonished looks, he continued. "It was most likely the house of a nobleman, perhaps Qist himself. Incan metallurgy was so advanced, they knew how to take the impurities out of gold and turn it into thin sheets that would reflect the sun. A house covered with gold would shine brightly, notifying people it belonged to an important nobleman. At the time Pizarro invaded the Incan Empire, the Europeans still hadn't developed that refining process."

"That's really neat!" Sophia stared into the yard imagining the scene. "A gold house!"

"They also made boats and islands out of bundles of reeds," Great Grandfather explained. "They were as skilled on the water as they were in the mountains. Reed boats are still in use today at Lake Titicaca in southern Peru. In fact, a British ship reportedly found an Incan reed boat 500 miles off the shore of South America, with a crew of 25, in the 17th century!"

The kids stared at him. "They made islands?"

"Look it up online. They tied big bundles of reeds together to make small floating islands in the lake for people to live on. They're still doing it today. They also developed the tomato."

Sophia blinked. "The tomato? Like you sell from your garden?"

"The very same! It spread from what we know as Peru all over the world."

"They certainly weren't savages, were they?" Juan shook his head.

"Not at all. They were capable of brutality in war, but they were far from savage in peaceful times. Which reminds me, how are you doing with the slings?"

Juan and Sophia exchanged glances.

"We have increased the distance to 20 yards." Juan explained. "It seems to work better than trying to throw 30 yards when we're so inexperienced." He smiled ruefully. "Sophia hit the can twice yesterday, but I only hit mine once."

"That's a good strategy," their relative said, nodding. "Build your accuracy first and the distance will come. I think you will see a lot of progress this next week."

CHAPTER 12
Descent

A BOLT OF PAIN in his left thigh jolted Adzul to consciousness. Another stab in his left calf caused him to lunge upright with a groan. At the motion, two huge birds squawked loudly and flapped heavily into the air from his side. Vultures! His body had been sprawled on the rocks for hours and they thought it was a corpse to feast on! Luckily, one arm had been thrown across his face or they would have plucked out his eyes with their first bite! As it was, one bird had pecked open the bullet wound and the second one had bitten a small hunk from his right leg. In addition, his entire torso ached from the beating at the hands of the soldiers. Pain in his scalp revealed lacerations to his gently probing fingers; the soldiers had used their sword handles as clubs after he went down.

The sun was more than halfway across the sky, but it gave precious little heat at this time of year. He was still wearing the tunic and armor shirt. Being made of wool, they had given him a bit of warmth while he slept in spite of being soaked. Now, however, the deadly cold would be his worst enemy until he could reach lower elevations. He stripped off both garments and wrung out every drop of water before putting them back on. He was relieved to see the sling still wrapped around his wrist, but the waterfall had torn off his sandals.

He could feel the temperature dropping; within an hour it would be well below zero, and there was not enough grass for a fire. He knew he would have to keep moving to stay alive. Scanning the cliffs, he saw no sign of the conquistadors. Most likely they were also out of food and were headed back to raid villages.

Although both feet were badly swollen from the impact on the water, his left ankle was so severely sprained that he could barely walk. Hobbling to the river's edge, he went down on hands and knees for a long drink. Resisting the urge to start down the mountain, he began to turn over rocks along the bank. Sure enough, there were grubs and beetles crawling under them. He eagerly devoured every one he could find. It wasn't much more than a mouthful, but he knew even that would give him energy for the ordeal ahead.

Stumbling painfully to where the rapids poured out of the pool, he studied the slope below. It stretched down as far as he could see, covered with dirt and rocks and so steep that standing upright would be almost impossible. An occasional boulder, seeming to defy gravity, perched in the soil and except for a random blade or two there was no grass or brush visible in the entire expanse. Glancing at the sky, he saw there was only an hour of daylight left. It was time to begin. He sat and eased himself off the edge of the flat area beside the pool. Extending his legs, with hands braced behind, he started down in sort of a crabwalk. Every movement sent arrows of pain throughout his battered body. *Took a tumble down the mt side - Beaten & Bloody*

For a few yards, Adzul was able to descend under control but the dirt and rock started to slide and he lost balance, rolling and tumbling head over heels in a mini-avalanche, completely unable to slow himself. In a cloud of dust, he slammed into a boulder 100 yards down the hill. The pain was so great that for a moment all he could do was lie there and gasp for breath.

When his breathing slowed, Adzul raised himself to a sitting position behind the boulder. His forehead had been gashed and blood was running off the tip of his nose. He checked himself but nothing appeared to be broken, although his arms and legs were bleeding in several places. He knew a serious injury would hamper his ability to get off the mountain, and that he had to be more careful in the future. Edging around the rock, he began the descent once more. This time he lay almost flat on his back and dug his heels into the dirt, arms and hands stretched to each side against the ground for further stability. In such a fashion, he was able to control his slide and make good time downhill. By the end of the afternoon, he was more than a quarter of a mile below the waterfall.

As darkness began to fall, he noted a boulder close to the raging rapids and steered himself to it on the avalanche of dirt under his body. From there it was only 3 or 4 yards to the water's edge, and he carefully negotiated the distance. After bathing his bruised hands and feet in the icy water, he took a long drink before starting a search for grubs. The rocks yielded three handfuls before he returned to the stability of the boulder.

For a while he sat on the uphill side of the rock, swinging his arms back and forth to stimulate circulation. As the temperature started to drop rapidly, he forced himself to stand on his battered feet. Holding the boulder to steady himself, he began to alternately raise and lower his knees to his chest until he could feel blood coursing through his legs. Hour after hour through the long night, he kept arms and legs moving to ward off the deadly cold. Many times he was tempted to sit down and sleep, but he knew if he gave in he would never rise again. Brilliant constellations slowly making their way across the frigid sky were the only witnesses to his struggle.

Finally, a band of red across the distant horizon signaled daybreak. Adzul was tottering with exhaustion. He had barely survived the night; the tips of his fingers and toes were white with frostbite, and he desperately needed food and sleep but didn't dare rest. As soon as there was enough light to see, he resumed his downhill slide. Skills learned the day before helped, and by noon he had managed almost a mile down the slope. With the sun at its highest point, he decided to stop for water and food. Steering himself to the river, he found a small pool. A determined search yielded several mouthfuls of grubs before he paused to drink.

As he raised his head from the water, a touch of color downstream caught Adzul's attention. Something unnatural covered the top of a rock jutting out of the current 70 yards away. Scrambling to the slope, he launched himself down. He had become rather adept in controlling his slide and came to a stop where he estimated the rock was located. Moving to the bank, he looked around. Ten feet below him was the rock, and on it was draped his wool cloak! He could hardly believe his eyes. The enraged soldiers must have thrown it in the river when they were beating him. Weariness evaporated with his excitement, and in minutes the lifesaving piece of clothing was in his hands.

CHAPTER 13

Survival

Adzul spent the next hour wringing every drop of moisture possible out of the cloak. He had been worried about staying awake during the coming night, but now he knew he wasn't going to freeze to death. Wrapped in the cloak, he could safely sleep. Starvation was the remaining enemy. He had to get to the tree line miles below before he would find food. With renewed determination, he continued his descent of the impossibly steep slopes.

In midafternoon, weakened by lack of food and exhaustion, he lost his footing while negotiating a small cliff and fell 15 feet. He landed on his side and rolled almost 60 yards down the hill in a cloud of dust and rocks. Fortunately, a boulder stopped him but he had suffered a laceration on the back of his head that bled profusely. After jamming part of the cloak against the wound until the bleeding ended, he decided that he could go no farther that day. His body was a mass of pain.

As the sun began to touch the top of the western mountains, Adzul struggled to the river but only found two or three grubs. Too tired to search any more, he curled up among the rocks and went to sleep wrapped in the heavy cloak. During the night, it began to snow.

The Incan opened his eyes to white. Eight inches of snow covered him! Although it had created additional insulation against the cold during the night, it was falling so heavily that he could literally see nothing. It seemed like he was in the middle of a thick fog. If the storm kept up, the snow would be too deep for travel within hours. Unable to move, he would die of starvation. He had to get started before it was too late.

Sleep had refreshed him enormously, but he was terribly weak from the wounds and lack of food. Making his way to the river, he took time to drink deeply before starting. Using his sling to tie the cloak firmly around himself he began his crablike descent, keeping the rushing river for a point of reference to the right. As the snow accumulated, he found it gave him the ability to slide more rapidly down the 45-degree slope but the cold was terrible on his exposed hands and feet.

On his back, with arms spread and feet lifted slightly above the surface of snow, he was soon speeding downhill at a rate that would have been impossible on the dirt. The only challenge was avoiding boulders, invisible in the whiteout. He would slam into them and tumble sideways for many yards before getting himself stopped. Once, he flew off a cliff and fell 30 feet into a snowbank. Although unhurt, it took him 40 minutes to dig his way out.

Hour after hour he slid, helped by the combination of deep snow and steep hillsides. In midafternoon, the snow gradually stopped falling and the clouds began to break up overhead. Cold sunlight showed a white landscape on every side, but in the far distance he could see the carpet of green stretching away to the east. The ground had started to flatten slightly and he was just able to stand upright, aided by the snow that came to his waist. He had managed to stay close to the river all day, and now he forced his way over to it for water.

On hands and knees, he overturned snow-covered rocks to expose treasures of grubs! He had come almost 5 miles down the mountain, and the insect life was more abundant at the lower altitude. For nearly an hour he foraged at the edge of the river, plucking bugs from the underside of rocks until he could find no more. Although the sum total was less than three dozen insects, it was enough to dull the pain in his stomach. With renewed strength, he slid and fought his way downhill for another hour before dusk.

Digging a hole in the snow, Adzul curled into a tight ball with the cloak pulled completely around him. Although the combined wool of his armor shirt, tunic, and cloak had kept his core temperature warm enough to prevent him from freezing, he was literally shaking with cold from the constant exposure of his limbs to snow during the long day. Gradually, his nearly frozen hands and feet began to warm, accompanied by severe pain as blood forced its way through tissue shrunk from cold. He was so tired that even the pain couldn't keep him awake for more than a few minutes.

In the morning, the sky was clear and it was bitterly cold. Testing the snow, he found the surface had frozen solid during the night. If he kept his body stretched out, he could slide on top without breaking through and within a short time was hurtling downhill! The snow was so deep only the tops of the biggest boulders poked up, and he was easily able to steer around them with his outstretched arms. The slopes had noticeably flattened, but the hard snow allowed him to fly downhill for several hours until the sun-softened snow caused him to flounder. When he could slide no more, he was surprised to find the snow less than knee deep. For the rest of the day, he hobbled steadily downhill.

The following morning the surface was frozen again, and he was able to make rapid progress. But after sliding for two hours, he began to encounter so many exposed rocks that he was forced to stop. The snow was just ankle deep and he was able to walk steadily down gentle slopes. An hour later, the snow gave way to brown grass and dirt. The air was chilly but the deep, biting cold had disappeared. Adzul was out of the high mountains.

CHAPTER 14
Rainforest

He kept moving, battered feet suffering with every step on the rocky soil, driven by the hunger that gnawed at his stomach. Sunken cheeks highlighted the dark hollows under his eyes. Under the armor shirt, every rib was showing. The awful bruises on his head and body from the conquistadors' beating had turned yellow, making his shriveled skin look like that of an old man. His arms and legs were terribly thin and he was literally tottering by the end of each day, but his eyes never left the vast green expanse rising to meet him. Only grubs and the riverwater kept him alive.

Four days after leaving the snow, Adzul encountered the scattered trees and shrubbery of the lower slopes. At sunset, two days later, he staggered into the rain forest and collapsed beside the trunk of a large tree along the river. He was half dead; if a predator had come on him that night, he would have been unable to defend himself. Oblivious to the hum of millions of insects and the intermittent shrieks from unseen night creatures, he sprawled on the ground more unconscious than asleep.

At dawn an unearthly roar caused his eyelids to fly open. It came again, so menacing that he dared not move for fear of being discovered. Too weak to fight, his only hope was to remain hidden so he searched his surroundings with his eyes for the source of the noise. Nothing moved. As he lay there, heart pounding, he realized the medallion was cool on his chest. He wondered whether it only warned him of human danger.

As minutes went by and the roar wasn't repeated, the warrior slowly pushed himself to a sitting position against the tree. He began to study his surroundings. It was a world diametrically opposed to the granite and snow of the Andes. Brilliant green hemmed him in on all sides in the growing daylight, accompanied by a cacophony of sound from bugs, birds, and animals all vocalizing simultaneously. High overhead, a canopy of leafy branches blocked sunlight from reaching the jungle floor. Impossibly tall trees were everywhere and huge butterflies fluttered among the vines and flowers that covered them. Colorful birds, large and small, darted among the foliage.

Movement in the canopy caught his attention. An animal was making its way slowly through the greenery; its body was about 3 feet in length and black. With long arms, and a tail at least as long as its body, it swung from branch to branch. Reaching a thick limb growing out of a tree trunk, it settled itself and then let out a roar that seemed to fill the forest! Flinching in spite of himself, Adzul realized this was the sound that had wakened him. No wonder the medallion had remained cool; the sound came from a monkey! He remembered relatives from the lowlands telling him as a boy about these animals. They called them "howler" monkeys.

At the sound, many smaller monkeys scattered with great leaps through the trees, surprised by the howler. He noticed that when the forest returned to normal some of these smaller monkeys descended close to the ground, searching for nuts and berries in bushes and low trees. The fruit would be food for him as well but, in his starved condition, the thought of meat was overpowering. He spotted a group of bushes nearly 50 yards away that attracted a number of monkeys. As he slowly stood up the animals scattered into the canopy, startled by the movement.

Dizzy and weak the warrior moved behind the tree, where hidden from sight he unwrapped the sling from his waist. Although the soft forest dirt offered no stones, the river was only a step away and he retrieved three rocks from the shallows. He loaded the sling with one rock and held the other two in his left hand.

He made his way to a large tree that he had noted 20 yards from the bushes. Standing with his back against it, he let the pouch rest on the ground and shortened his grip on the straps. He knew there wouldn't be enough time to swing the full 5-foot length of the sling before the monkeys raced out of range. He might be able to throw in time by using only 3 feet of strap.

The monkeys were 90 feet in the air perched on branches in the canopy, watching him. He knew if he remained absolutely still they would finally lose interest, and he was counting on some of them returning to the fruit-bearing bushes. The problem was his physical condition. The ambush required him to be absolutely still until the monkeys saw him only as part of the tree. That might take hours, and he wasn't sure that his strength would hold out.

Within 30 minutes the animals lost interest in the figure below and resumed swinging through the tree-tops, but none of them showed signs of approaching the bushes. After an hour, Adzul's legs began to quiver and he was only able to keep from falling by the utmost effort of willpower. When two hours had gone by, with no evidence that the monkeys would return, he began to think of going to the bushes and eating the fruit himself. He was about to step away from the tree when he saw three big howlers begin to make their way out of the canopy.

At first it seemed like they were headed in another direction, but ever so slowly they adjusted their descent toward the bushes in front of him. After 30 minutes they finally reached the cluster and began plucking fruit, occasionally glancing in his direction. Adzul kept his eyes averted, trying to watch them with peripheral vision so as not to make eye contact. Ten minutes later, the opportunity presented itself. One of the three turned in such a way that its back was toward him. It was time to strike.

Forcing his cramped muscles to move, Adzul took two quick steps away from the trunk and set the shortened sling whistling around his head. The instant he moved, the monkeys screeched and rushed upward toward the protection of the canopy. Two had a head start because they were facing him; the third was behind because it hadn't seen the motion and was reacting to the screams of the others. That delay was fatal. The rock, thrown with only two swings, struck the back of its head with a crunch, cutting off its screeches abruptly. The body fell out of the branches in a lazy arc to the forest floor. In a flash the man was on it, with another rock raised in his fist, but the monkey was dead. In practically no time, the body was skinned and roasting over a fire.

CHAPTER 15
Failure

"**I** DID IT!" Sophia yelled one morning. "Bull's-eye!" Her aluminum can had jumped backward through the air after a direct hit.

Juan came running. "How did it feel?"

"Smooth. I let the sling do the work and just concentrated on release point and following through."

"That's what Great Grandfather said," Juan commented thoughtfully. "We don't have the arm strength to muscle the rock through the air for 30 yards, but the centrifugal force of the sling will do it easily. I've been just missing the can this morning, but every throw has plenty of power." He returned to his position, determined to acquire the accuracy. A few minutes later, a triumphant shout indicated that he had succeeded!

It took three more weeks of concentrated practice before they felt confident enough to announce to Great Grandfather that they had mastered the sling.

"Show me," he responded. It was another beautiful Saturday morning.

Juan grabbed a small stump from the woodpile out back and set it up across the street, beside the tree where the old man had buried his rock. On top of it, he set an empty Coke can. He moved well away while Sophia loaded her sling. Swinging it easily, she let the centrifugal force build through five revolutions, the pouch whistling through the air. The rock was a blur when she threw it. It hit the can squarely in the middle, knocking it 10 feet through the air and splitting both sides completely open!

Great Grandfather smiled. "Well done!"

With Juan supplying new cans for each throw, Sophia repeated the feat four more times. Her relative was impressed.

"How long have you been at it?" he asked. "About 10 weeks?"

"No, it's just eight weeks since we began practicing."

"That's extremely good progress," he complimented her. "Normally it takes a good deal more time to develop that much strength and accuracy."

"We threw for a couple of extra hours on Saturdays and Sundays," Juan offered as Sophia went to set up the first target for him. "We never missed a day!"

Juan's first four throws smashed the cans just as Sophia's had. Each can flew back as if jet propelled, split wide open! On the last throw, he decided to give Great Grandfather a special treat and knock the can twice as far. Cranking the sling with all his might on the last two revolutions, he let it fly. To his horror, the can only wobbled slightly as the rock zinged by to the right, missing it by a millimeter. In shocked silence, he turned to Great Grandfather.

"You know, the sling will do the work for us, if we just let it." The voice was gentle. "Trying to add anything takes away from its accuracy. But you two are doing much better than I expected! Keep up the good work. By the way, are you keeping the sling with you at all times?"

"Yes, sir," they replied. "It's wrapped around our waists when we aren't practicing, just the way you told us."

"Excellent! It's unlikely, but you might need them sometime." He turned to Juan, "A little more practice and I know you'll get it."

The boy tried to hide his disappointment. "I'll have two weeks of throwing in by the next time we see you because Dad wants to take us to the mountains next weekend."

Sophia stared at Great Grandfather as they settled on the porch in front of him. "There must be a good reason for you wanting us to be so accurate."

He only smiled. "Two weeks it is. I should probably hold both of you to 10 out of 10 hits by then." The old man chuckled as he rocked back to continue the story.

CHAPTER 16

Recovery

FOR THE NEXT THREE WEEKS Adzul remained by the river, hunting monkeys and harvesting nuts and fruit from the rain forest. Gradually his emaciated body began to fill out and regain its muscular shape. Monkey skins were cured and fashioned into sandals and a pouch for sling rocks. The wool cloak, which had saved his life on the mountain, was turned into a large sack to carry food and supplies. A black-and-white headband, made from the skin of a monkey, replaced the red one that had been torn off by the waterfall. It was completed with two colorful feathers from a toucan, extending up in the warrior's 'V' in the front. The heat was so oppressive that he took off the armor shirt, but it was always close at hand in the sack. Although Adzul saw no evidence of other humans, he slept in a different location every night relying on the medallion to alert him if danger approached.

At the beginning of the fourth week, he left the river and headed north with a sack full of dried monkey meat and fruit. His strength had returned and the ugly scars on his thigh and feet were the only reminders of the ordeal he had been through.

Travel was slow through the profusion of trees, vines, and bushes that covered the forest floor. In the mountains he had been accustomed to seeing for miles, but now his vision was restricted to a few yards in any direction by the dense green growth. Heat and humidity, which had been so welcome after the bitter cold of the Andes, surrounded him like a giant steam bath. The constant noise of the jungle made him long for the silence of the high valleys.

One thing Adzul came to love about the rain forest was its variety of butterflies. They were everywhere, fluttering about the undergrowth. They combined with the parrots and toucans to give splashes of color against the solid green of the foliage. Some had light brown wings, edged in black, with large white spots set in the brown. Others had brilliant blue wings and still others had black wings with a large yellow spot in the middle. He stopped frequently to enjoy one of them sitting on a leaf, its wings slowly waving back and forth.

From time to time, he was wakened in the dark of night by a loud roar. It was different from that of the howler monkeys, who generally gave voice at dawn, deeper and more menacing. It would bring him abruptly to his feet, sling in hand. At such times the medallion felt slightly warm and he would rekindle his small fire, sitting well away from it with his back against a tree. If anything approached the light, he would be able to see it but would himself be invisible in the dark. Brave though he was, stories stirred in his memory about traders who had mysteriously disappeared in these same jungles.

One day as he was moving along the edge of a swamp, a loud squealing broke out just ahead and the medallion grew warm. He stopped immediately, but the thick undergrowth prevented him from seeing the cause of the noise. Advancing slowly he saw bushes shaking to the right, accompanied by more squeals. Gradually the sounds grew weaker until there was a loud crunch and they suddenly stopped. A step or two more revealed a 150-pound capybara lying on its side in shallow water, its entire body encased by two greenish brown coils as thick as Adzul's thigh. As he watched, the coils began to move and he realized they belonged to an enormous snake! The water stirred and a great head, with an open mouth full of wicked teeth, rose up. The snake grabbed the capybara's snout and began to push its jaws forward inch by inch. The jaws expanded wider and wider until they began to cover the rodent's entire head! When the head and neck had disappeared into the snake's body, Adzul shivered and backed away. From that time on, he was extremely cautious when traveling through swamps!

CHAPTER 17
The Basin

As the story ended, Juan was shaking his head. "I can't imagine what one of those snakes would do to a human. It was an anaconda, right?"

Great Grandfather nodded. "You don't want to let one of them get a coil wrapped around your body. It would mean the end of you! Fortunately, they take a long time to digest their prey so they are not always on the prowl."

"What's a capybara?' Sophia asked.

"It is a large rodent that has long reddish brown fur; it sort of looks like a hairy pig. It is not common in the high Andes but found at lower altitudes near water. Adzul would have called it a 'ronsoco.' Another animal of the rain forest is the tapir. It has short gray hair and a long flexible nose that it wraps around branches to strip off leaves. Oddly, it has four toes on the front feet and three on the back feet. A wooly version of this animal does live in the high Andes and Adzul would have been familiar with it."

She was curious. "Were there people living in the rainforest then?"

"Great question. We used to believe the Amazon Basin was largely uninhabited except for a few very primitive people; however, modern research now estimates there may have been millions living there during Adzul's time. It is true that rainforest soil is poor for growing crops, but there is evidence early peoples learned how to fertilize it in a variety of ways, among which was adding charcoal from cooking fires. There are more and more indications that large communities were scattered throughout the Basin. In fact, remains have been found of elevated causeways built through the swamps allowing people to travel between communities. Archeologists are beginning to believe these population centers had active trade and commerce with each other. Although the area of the Amazon Basin is enormous, the hundreds of rivers in it would have allowed travel between cities that were far apart."

"Have they found ruins?"

"Not many because the buildings were undoubtedly made from wood, which disintegrates rapidly in a tropical climate."

"What happened to all those people?"

"The tragedy of Europeans discovering the Americas is that diseases like smallpox, typhus, and cholera were introduced to people who had no natural immunity. It's now estimated that millions upon millions of people in both North and South America died of these diseases within decades after Columbus arrived. Populations in the Amazon would have been no exception. Probably the vast majority of them were wiped out and their cities reclaimed by the jungle."

Sophia persisted, "Didn't any of the early explorers in the Amazon encounter people before the diseases arrived?"

"Actually, one of Pizarro's officers descended into the Basin and traveled down the Amazon River all the way to the sea. There was a friar, or priest, in the party who recorded they passed many cities built on the banks. The people were so hostile, however, the Spaniards didn't dare stop." He grinned at the girl. "He even reported encountering a fierce population of women warriors! But it was scores of years before serious explorations took place, and by then the original populations were gone. Only a few remote villages remained, giving rise to the theory that the area was too inhospitable for humans."

He continued. "There has also been a legend for centuries about a lost city of gold in the Amazon. Dozens of people, using the most sophisticated equipment available, have died in the last 100 years searching for it."

"Modern people?" Juan was incredulous.

"Yes. The climate and jungle can be very dangerous. President Teddy Roosevelt nearly lost his life exploring an unknown river in the Amazon in 1913. His death, a few years later, was caused by an infection incurred during that trip." Great Grandfather smiled. "As you will see, the jungle was not easy for Adzul either."

dangers
of the
Amazon

CHAPTER 18

Encounter

IT WAS MIDAFTERNOON a week later when the medallion suddenly got hot! Adzul froze and peered through the dense foliage, his eyes the only part of him moving. Minutes went by before slight movement 30 yards ahead caught his attention. A man was crouched there with his back to the warrior, intent on something in front of him. His right arm drawing back the string of a 5-foot bow had caused the movement. He had brown skin and black hair trimmed close to his head. His muscular body was naked except for a loincloth. Suddenly he released the string, appearing to fire a long arrow straight into the ground ahead of him. Adzul wondered whether the target was one of the enormous snakes.

The man took a step forward, bent down and rose with the arrow clenched in his fist. On the end of it wriggled a large fish! Almost immediately, two other men materialized from the greenery and gave him congratulatory claps on the back. Adzul could hear all three talking as they disappeared among the trees to the left. He continued to stand motionless, all senses straining to discover whether the surrounding forest hid more people. After 45 minutes the medallion had cooled slightly, and he decided it was safe to move. Before taking a step, he slipped the sack from his back and donned his armor shirt. Its protection gave him a sense of security, but the continuing warmth of the silver reminded him to be careful.

Slipping forward, he discovered the man had been standing at the edge of a wide brown river that stretched more than a quarter of a mile to the far shore. As he watched from a hidden position in the foliage, several canoes passed on the way downstream. The men paddling were well armed, the ends of their bows and arrows showing above the sides of the craft. Adzul knew these people were not friendly because the medallion grew hot as soon as each canoe appeared.

Turning from the river, he retraced his steps into the jungle for a good distance before continuing upstream parallel to the river. He had not gone far when the faint smell of wood smoke came to his nostrils, indicating there was a community nearby. He judged it would be alongside the river and hoped he was far enough back in the forest to escape detection. He moved slowly, stopping frequently to search the undergrowth ahead. Although he was but a shadow moving noiselessly in the dense greenery, he knew others could do the same and he had to rely on the medallion to warn him of danger.

He heard the sound of voices just as the silver got hot! An opening appeared in the green wall of foliage and through it he caught a glimpse of cleared fields. Sliding closer, he observed a number of people working in large garden plots. It seemed there was a sizeable population nearby; indeed, a cloud of smoke lay in the direction of the river. It was close to dusk and people were leaving the fields and heading toward the river, their work done for the day.

Adzul changed his tactics and moved as rapidly as he could during the remaining hour of daylight. He realized he had to bypass the city as quickly as possible in order to remain undetected by the many people in the area. That night he slept uneasily at the foot of a tree, covering himself with large green leaves for camouflage. The medallion remained warm, a constant reminder of peril, and he was on his way at the first predawn gray.

He kept to the deep forest until the smell of smoke was completely gone and the medallion had grown cool. He then changed direction and began to move back toward the river. He had noted a path beside the water where the fisherman was hunting, and he guessed there would be a similar path upstream that would allow him to move rapidly away from the city. He knew the medallion would alert him to anyone approaching.

In late afternoon he caught sight of the muddy water and, sure enough, there was a good path running along the bank. The medallion had become slightly warmer so he waited many minutes before emerging from cover, thinking it was warning him of river traffic. When it didn't get hot, he finally stepped onto the path and began trotting steadily upstream. Within 20 minutes the silver had cooled, and he pressed on faster through the fading light.

Intent on studying the river for canoes, Adzul had failed to look up before starting along the path. He missed the small boy watching him from high above, hidden in the branches of a tall tree. The boy was there to collect honey from beehives hanging on the slender limbs where adults couldn't climb. He had been just about to knock down a large hive when the man appeared. Filled with excitement, he observed the Incan warrior disappear up the river. He would be well rewarded for reporting an enemy!

CHAPTER 19
Ambush!

IT WAS MIDMORNING the following day when the
medallion suddenly began to heat up. Adzul immediately stopped and moved behind a tree to study
the trail behind him. Nothing moved in the dense
greenery. Since setting foot on the trail, he had main-
tained a steady jog to put as much distance as possible
between him and the city. He was sure he had escaped
detection and wondered whether canoe traffic was
causing the warning. When nothing appeared on the
water, he decided to pick up the pace and try to leave
the threat behind. Breaking into an easy run that ate
up the miles, he sped along the path at a rate that he
could never have achieved in the forest.

By late afternoon the medallion had cooled, and he believed he was safe again. Nevertheless, with night approaching, he drew well back into the jungle and gathered a supply of giant 3-foot leaves. Finding a tangle of vines at the bottom of a large tree, he crept in among them and covered himself completely with the leaves. He went to sleep immediately, satisfied that in the black of night he would be invisible even to a predator.

Hours later Adzul's eyes flew open. It was pitch dark and the medallion was burning his chest! For the first time in his experience, the rainforest was quiet; night creatures had gone silent sensing danger. He lay motionless under the leaves, trying to detect the menace with his ears and nose. Long minutes passed with every instinct screaming that he was in mortal peril, but he knew moving would reveal his position and expose him to attack.

Then he heard it! Something had scraped on a leaf no more than 2 feet away, after which there was dead silence. Whatever it was had stopped moving and was waiting, motionless, beside him. He smelled sweat. A man was crouched there, a man who was hunting him! For what seemed like an eternity he lay, hardly daring to breathe. At last there was the faint sound of a vine shifting and the smell was gone. For the next two hours, the medallion remained hot and twice he heard faint sounds close by which told him there was more than one man searching the forest.

Gradually, the chorus of the night dwellers resumed and the medallion cooled as the hunters moved away. When faint gray light began to filter among the trees, he carefully extricated himself from the leaves and vines. Moving as carefully as he knew how, the warrior became a shadow flitting from cover to cover in the direction of the river. He found the trail and began moving along it, increasing speed with the growing light until he was in a full run. Adzul thought he might outrun the hunters, but part of him suspected that they wouldn't give up.

It was midmorning when the heat of the medallion warned him the men behind were near. Adzul paused for a moment to don the armor shirt and then sped on but the medallion grew hotter. The hunters could run too! When the silver began to burn, he knew they were so close behind that he had to make a stand. Sprinting ahead to give himself as much separation as possible, he searched for anything to give him an advantage in the coming fight.

Suddenly, an opening in the forest appeared to his left. It was about half the size of a football field and was covered with grass and low bushes. It had been cleared at one time for planting, but the jungle was reclaiming it. He raced to the very middle and turned to face his pursuers, loaded sling whirling through the air. Nothing appeared on the trail and the solid wall of vegetation around the clearing was still, but the medallion was so hot he knew the men were there. His body was covered with sweat from running in the terrific heat and humidity of the jungle but the monkey-skin headband absorbed the salty moisture, keeping his dark eyes clear as he studied the greenery and waited.

Without warning six long arrows materialized in the air, striking him in the chest and sides! The impact staggered him and it was a moment before he regained his stance, sling still spinning. One by one the arrows fell harmlessly to the ground, leaving only a black spot where each had struck the armor cloth. A minute before there had been nothing but a green wall in front of him, but now six men stood less than 20 yards away. Black paint marked their faces and their teeth were filed to sharp points. Each had a bow, which was almost longer than they were tall, drawn back with an arrow aimed at him. No one moved for a moment until Adzul suddenly started advancing toward them!

In confusion the men backed up a step and began talking excitedly to each other, never taking their eyes off the stranger who was now walking forward swinging a rope around his head. They could clearly see the marks where their poisoned arrows had struck his body, but the arrows lay on the ground and he was showing no effect from the deadly curare. By now, he should be writhing on the ground in his death throes. Suddenly their leader grunted and dropped his bow, his left arm broken between the elbow and shoulder.

The Incan warrior had decided the best strategy was to go on the attack after the armor shirt rendered the arrows harmless. As he strode forward, he noticed one of the men was slightly taller and the others seemed to be glancing in his direction for guidance. He guessed the tall one was the leader and fired at his arm without breaking stride. The hurtling rock broke the humerus like a twig! As the rest of the men stared at their war chief in dismay, Adzul reloaded the sling and set it swinging. He stopped 10 yards from the group and stared at them with implacable eyes.

The uncertain warriors darted glances between Adzul and their leader. With his left arm hanging uselessly at his side, the chief looked at the stranger and barked out a command. Adzul had already targeted the bridge of the man's nose for his next rock, which would have sent splinters of bone into the brain killing him instantly, but he hesitated because all the men dropped their bows and fell face down on the ground! After a minute or two they backed slowly into the wall of green, murmuring in a strange singsong manner. Before he could decide what to do next, they reappeared on hands and knees, heads bowed, pushing woven bags along the ground in front of them.

He realized the bags were filled with supplies to sustain them during the chase and they were making an offering to him. He suspected they had not seen the rock leave the sling and believed he had broken the chief's arm by the same magic that saved him from the arrows. He stopped whirling the sling and tucked it behind his back, not wanting them to understand that it was quite ordinary. Spreading his legs and putting hands on his waist, he assumed a fierce pose and grunted. The leader cautiously raised his head. Speaking loudly in the Incan tongue, Adzul accompanied it with universal sign language.

"I was traveling peacefully through your country, but you decided to pursue me. My great magic protected me and wounded you. In return for these gifts, I will not harm you further if you return immediately to your city. Do not come back or all of you will die!"

The leader muttered something and they backed away, disappearing into the greenery. Within 20 minutes, the medallion was completely cool; the men had gone. Collecting what food he could use, Adzul added it to his own sack and threw the rest into the jungle where it would be devoured by insects and creatures within 24 hours. The bows and arrows were broken into pieces and buried in the soft earth. Satisfied that all evidence of the encounter had been removed, he returned to the path and continued his journey north.

CHAPTER 20
Diego

G REAT GRANDFATHER was startled by a knock on the door at 8:00 Sunday morning. Usually his vegetable customers didn't start appearing before 10:00. He opened the front door to see the excited faces of Juan and Sophia!

"I thought you were camping in the mountains," he exclaimed.

"Great Grandfather, you will never believe what happened!" Juan was almost shouting. "We had to come back because of Diego's wounds, but it's amazing how everything you said came true!"

"Diego's wounds?"

"Yes, but he's OK," Sophia interjected. "We have to tell you what happened!"

Seeing the twins were not to be denied, he smiled and waved them inside. "All right, let's hear it. But first, have you had breakfast?"

After being assured they had, he went to the kitchen and put glasses of milk and a platter of their favorite chocolate chip cookies on the table. Sitting back in his chair sipping coffee, he waited patiently while they dived into the cookies.

"Gotta have one cookie before we start," Juan said, munching happily. "OK. We left yesterday morning on schedule, planning to get back this evening. Dad wanted to go up above Del Norte to that hunting camp on the stream; you know, the one where he shot that huge bull elk about four years ago."

Great Grandfather nodded; he knew exactly the spot Juan was talking about.

"Well, we got to the stream just before lunch. The forest was really beautiful and the meadow where we always set up the tents looked like no one had been there since last hunting season. Sophia and I helped unload the pickup and set up the tent, then we grabbed our fly rods and headed for the stream."

Dad had introduced the twins to fly-fishing when they were 5 years old. There was nothing they liked better than seeing the splash of a trout attacking the fly they had delicately floated past its nose! Great Grandfather smiled proudly because he knew not many adults could drop a fly as softly onto a pool, in the middle of bushes, as these kids could.

"The brookies were really hungry and we caught a ton of them without having to move very far. We kept a couple for supper and released all the rest back into the stream. After about an hour, Mom called us for lunch. She had brought chicken enchiladas wrapped in foil, which we heated over the fire. Then she broke out a pie that she had made with your strawberries, Great Grandfather! It was awesome! While we were finishing it, we noticed that Diego was gone."

Diego was the family dog. He was small, brown and white, with floppy ears and a short tail. There was nothing he liked better than a trip to the country and he had been a pest all morning while they were loading the truck, leaping and jumping about, constantly barking. Only when they were under way did he settle down on Sophia's lap and fall asleep.

"He had been with us at the stream," Juan continued. "But we lost track of him when we came back to camp. I was just starting to call him when we heard a high-pitched scream from back in the forest."

"It sounded like a baby!" Sophia burst in. "In an instant, I realized it was Diego and Juan and I dropped our pies and raced into the forest toward the sound. As we ran, there was another scream and we heard growling. We came to a clearing and there was Diego, surrounded by three coyotes. He was on the ground and one of them had his back leg in its mouth. Another, with blood on its jaws, had just bitten him deep on his shoulder. The third was crouched over him, about to bury its fangs in his throat!"

"Sophia screamed 'slings,' and I yelled at them at the top of my lungs," Juan continued. "That probably saved Diego's life because the first coyote immediately started pulling him toward the trees. The others stopped to look at us and when they turned back, Diego had been dragged about 3 feet away. In the meantime, we ripped the slings from our waists and loaded them in record time. The third coyote made one jump and dove in for the kill. My first rock hit its head just before its jaws locked onto Diego's neck. There was a loud 'crunch' and it dropped instantly!"

Sophia picked up the story. "I aimed at the animal that was dragging Diego toward the trees. My rock hit it between the eyes and it slumped over like it'd been struck with a sledgehammer! The last one turned and ran, but just as it reached the trees Juan's second shot sliced the tail off its body like a knife! It disappeared, howling with pain."

The kids had rushed to the side of their stricken pet. There was blood everywhere and he was in shock. Had they arrived a minute later, he would have been dead. Juan tenderly picked him up and they headed for camp. Diego was laid gently on a blanket and Dad carefully cleaned the blood from his wounds. In addition to the shoulder and leg, he had been bitten on his back and left side.

After anxious moments, Dad rendered his verdict. "There are puncture wounds and lacerations and nothing seems broken, but we should get him down to the vet for bandaging and antibiotics. We'll have to put off the camping trip for another time, but it looks like all your practice with the slings paid off. You just saved Diego's life!"

A thought suddenly struck Juan. "Dad, did your father ever teach you to use the sling?"

His father smiled as he folded the blanket over the little dog and stood up. He lifted his shirt and neatly wrapped around his stomach were the unmistakable braided leather strings of a sling. He nodded at their mother and she revealed an identical weapon wrapped around her slim waist!

"I don't believe it!" Sophia was astonished. It had never occurred to her that their parents might be armed.

"We have hardly ever had to use them," Dad explained. "We do practice. For 500 years, everyone in the immediate family has known how to use the sling. It's an important part of the family tradition. But let's get packed up and head for the vet."

When the twins finished, Great Grandfather smiled. "Now you understand why I set such a high standard of accuracy. Often there's only time for one throw."

CHAPTER 21
Shirts

GREAT GRANDFATHER was quiet for a few moments. Finally, he turned to the twins. "Perhaps I was a bit hasty about your accuracy with the sling, Juan. True skill always comes out under real pressure. I think you passed the test with Diego. The two of you have earned the right to wear one of the greatest Incan inventions."

The twins stared at him blankly, racking their brains to remember inventions from the Incan Empire. Sophia finally ventured, "Something made from wool?"

"Yes, but not to keep you warm." He disappeared into a room off the kitchen, returning with what looked like two gray sleeveless shirts. He handed one to Juan.

"Put it on." The shirt was thicker than a regular T-shirt and form-fitting, ending just below the boy's waist. Pinching the smooth hem, he looked questioningly at the old man.

"Sophia, poke him hard in the chest with your finger," Great Grandfather ordered. She stepped in front of her brother and poked him in the chest with a stiff forefinger.

"Harder!" the old man urged.

She gave Juan a much harder poke.

"That's funny, I don't feel a thing."

Great Grandfather reached down to a toolbox on the floor and pulled out a heavy hammer. "Hit him with that."

Sophia's eyes grew wide. "Really?"

"Yes, you won't hurt him."

The girl tapped her brother lightly on the chest with the hammer.

"Harder."

She swung the hammer slightly harder.

"Juan, did you feel anything?" Great Grandfather's tone of voice indicated that he already knew the answer.

"Nope, nothing."

"Again," Great Grandfather ordered. "But harder this time!"

Sophia swung the tool moderately hard against Juan's chest. He swayed slightly from the impact but indicated again that he felt nothing.

"Hit him as hard as you can!" He turned to Juan. "Brace yourself."

The boy put one foot behind him and leaned slightly forward.

Sophia was scared. "Are you sure this won't hurt him?"

"I promise. You know I wouldn't do anything to hurt either one of you."

"OK. Here goes!" With that, Sophia reared back and grabbed the hammer with both hands, swinging it at her brother with all her strength. With a dull "thud" the hammer hit him squarely in the chest!

There was silence for an instant. Sophia was wide-eyed with fear. Great Grandfather smiled with satisfaction.

"That's absolutely amazing! I felt the force of the hammer hitting the shirt, but there's no pain or feeling at all in my chest!" Juan was excited. "What the heck is this shirt anyway?"

"It's an Incan armor shirt, one of their extraordinary creations," Great Grandfather explained. "Their cloth armor could take the slash of a sword, or the thrust of a lance, almost as effectively as the steel armor of the conquistadors. Repeated heavy blows would bruise the skin, as they did with Adzul, but could not break bones. In fact, this armor was so easy to wear in battle that many conquistadors abandoned their clumsy gear and adopted it for themselves! The original design was rather thick but our ancestor, Qist, improved the weave to make the shirt much thinner without losing any of its strength. He taught Adzul the new weave and commanded him to make sure it was passed on to each generation of the family. I learned it from my father and your parents will teach it to you."

"It's a little thicker than a sweatshirt, but it could certainly pass for one that's had the arms cut off." Juan fingered the material.

"These shirts are to be used for protection." Great Grandfather handed the second one to Sophia. "You don't need to wear them every day, of course, but the time may come when they will be useful." *foreshadowing*

CHAPTER 22

Attack!

FOR WEEKS ADZUL SAW no further evidence of humans until, beyond the end of the Andes, he reencountered the ancient trail used by the traders. He welcomed the ease of travel it provided and progressed steadily northward. One day several weeks later, he came to a large cleared area the size of 10 soccer fields. In the middle was a huge, flat-topped, four-sided pyramid at least 60 feet high made from large blocks of rock. It had obviously been abandoned and grass and brush were beginning to cover it. He stood in the protection of the trees, studying it for almost an hour. The side facing him had wide stairs going all the way to the top, but at the bottom the stairs split around a large rectangular doorway in the pyramid's base.

All was still in the midday sun. The medallion remained cool, so the warrior was reasonably certain that there was no danger; however, he was cautious because there might still be people in the area and he wanted to avoid a chance encounter until he could observe them. He began a careful circuit of the temple, remaining within the safety of the trees. Each side of the structure had stairs going to the top, but there were no other doorways. Returning to his starting point, the warrior was satisfied the temple was deserted. He was curious to learn whether this doorway led to food storerooms for priests in the same manner as the Incan temples. Anything left behind would be a welcome change from his diet of monkey meat.

As a precaution, he slipped the armor shirt from his sack and put it on. He also unwrapped the sling and loaded it, shortening his grip on the straps until they were 3-feet long. This would allow him to use it within a confined space without sacrificing much power. Leaving his sack beside a tree, he stepped into the open with the sling hanging from his right hand and slowly approached the doorway. It was 8-feet high and 12-feet wide, with an enormous stone lintel across the top. Sunlight slanted in to reveal a few feet of stone floor, but beyond was darkness. Once inside, he stopped to let his eyes adjust to the dim light.

The hallway stretched straight ahead and there seemed to be faint light at its far end. The air smelled musty and damp, and dust and cobwebs covered the walls. Filtered sunlight revealed dozens of bats hanging from the ceiling; it seemed no people had been there for a long time. He moved forward slowly, his sandals making no sound on the dirt covering the stone floor.

At the end of the hall, Adzul peered into a large room beneath the apex of the pyramid. Shafts in the ceiling extended through the rock to the open air, letting in faint light. Thick pillars held the weight of the structure above, although portions of the ceiling had begun to collapse and there were piles of rubble on the floor. He wondered whether this was the reason for the pyramid being abandoned. As he scanned the walls, he saw no doorways and gave up hope of finding food in an overlooked storeroom.

Suddenly, out of the corner of his eye, he picked up movement on the other side of the room! Something had darted across the floor between piles of rock. As he stared it moved again, covering distance with incredible speed to disappear behind another rock mound closer to him. The hair on the back of his neck began to prickle, and the medallion grew hot under the armor shirt. There was danger, and it was time to get out into the open!

Backing swiftly down the hall, Adzul kept his eyes focused on the entrance to the room and started whirling the sling. Just as he reached the sunlight he thought he saw something appear at the far end of the passage, but it was indistinct due to the bright light now assaulting his eyes. As he continued to back away from the temple, he let the sling extend to its full 5-foot length. The familiar swish of the weapon was comforting as he focused on the opening, not knowing what to expect. He was 30 feet away when the attack came.

With a bloodcurdling roar, an animal shot out of the doorway at him with unbelievable speed. There was no time to fire the sling! Two hundred pounds of fury hit him full in the chest and he staggered, falling on his back. Needle-sharp hooked claws slammed into his armor shirt, entangling themselves in the material. A snarling mouth with fearsome teeth lunged at his face, but by thrusting both hands out he managed to grab the animal by the throat and hold it off. Desperately struggling to defend himself, a name flashed in his mind from his father's stories: Jaguar!

Fortunately for Adzul, the cat could not free its claws from the tight fibers of the armor shirt or the battle would have ended quickly. It could only strain its head toward his face and neck and strike at his body with its rear legs. Deep wounds that bled profusely were torn into the man's thighs and legs by the claws of the animal's back feet. The warrior's arms, corded with straining muscles, were all that prevented the jaguar from killing him.

Adzul frantically tried to roll to his left, but the animal repositioned its back legs to keep him pinned to the ground. For a moment it was a standoff, but the fight was beginning to take its toll. In spite of his determination, the wounds and the sheer strength of the animal were weakening the warrior. His arms started to bend and the cat pressed the attack by forcing its head closer, snarling viciously, hot stinking breath blasting the man's face.

He knew the end was near. His arms were now bent at almost right angles, and he had to push his head backward to stay away from the teeth. With one last titanic effort, Adzul raised his body off the ground and tried to shove the jaguar away. For a moment they were poised, the Incan half sitting and the cat digging its back feet into the ground to force him back down. In that instant, he felt the cat's body jerk hard to the left. It recovered immediately, snarling ferociously and straining at him but with what seemed to be less strength. There was a second violent jerk and the animal slumped over and then rolled completely off him, its muscles relaxing and eyes losing focus. It was dead.

Totally spent, the warrior sat slumped with his chin on his chest, a deep weariness flooding his entire body. At length, he was able to pry the claws out of his armor shirt and thrust the cat's legs away from him, startled to see two spears buried deep in its side. He rolled onto his hands and knees and tried to stand, but his legs didn't seem to work and he pitched forward face first. The last thing he saw before losing consciousness was a young woman standing beside him with a spear in her hand.

CHAPTER 23
The Girl

A LOUD NOISE INTRUDED into Adzul's nightmare. He was struggling with a huge beast and knew he was going to die; its yellow eyes gleamed in triumph. In a minute it would be over. Then the beast was gone and he was under water drowning, held down by enormous pressure. Suddenly a human face appeared, contorted with rage, blood pouring from its head and its mouth open in a hideous shriek. The loud noise sounded again, pulling him away from these discordant images. Dawning consciousness brought with it pain that forced a moan from his lips. The loud sound was repeated, causing his eyes to open and memory to flood his brain. It was night and something was burning his chest!

There was a small fire flickering near his feet. On the other side of it crouched a girl, staring across the flames into the darkness. Her right arm was cocked backward holding a 3-foot stick, into a notch at the end of which was braced the butt of a spear. Her other hand balanced the shaft of the spear, which was fitted with a wicked-looking black obsidian point.

A snarling roar drew his eyes to the left; it was the same sound that had wakened him. A large jaguar crouched on the ground 20 feet away, yellow eyes highlighted by the fire, and with another roar it leaped directly at him. The man was powerless to get out of the way but the girl reacted instantly. Her right arm was a blur as it drove the stick forward, launching the spear. It hit the beast in midair, piercing its neck with such force that it knocked the cat into the bushes at the side of the fire. Thrashing, snapping, and growling erupted from the undergrowth and then the cat was up and springing at the girl. But she was ready, having grabbed a second spear and fitted it to the stick with lightning speed. She hurled the shaft at point-blank range into the jaguar's throat, severing arteries that fed its brain. It fell into the fire scattering sparks and ashes, letting dark reclaim the camp.

When Adzul woke again it was daytime. He lay for a while collecting himself, intense pain radiating from his legs. The fire had been rebuilt and the dead jaguar dragged out of camp. The girl was sitting across the flames working on a piece of its skin. As he stared up into the green foliage, images began to fill his mind. He relived the attack outside the pyramid and the sudden death of the jaguar as it was about to kill him. He remembered being roused from time to time to drink from a bowl and his wounds being treated with salve and poultices. Then came the second attack at the fire. The girl had saved his life twice!

With face set against the pain, he lifted his head and shoulders and pushed himself backward to a tree where he was able to sit up. The girl brought him a wooden bowl filled with water and inspected his legs while he drank. They were wrapped in strips of cotton, dark with dried blood. After satisfying herself that they had not started bleeding, she brought him a bowl of maize and several strips of dried meat. He found that he was ravenously hungry and finished every scrap. She smiled and brought him more.

In spite of his condition, he could not help noticing her. She was slender and moved with a gracefulness that belied her intensity with the spears. Shining black hair framed a beautiful face with large brown eyes and white teeth. She wore a white cotton shirt and matching knee-length pants.

"A lovely woman with the courage and skill of a warrior," he thought to himself as he fell asleep again.

Although he was weak from loss of blood, Adzul began to improve under the girl's care. He soon realized that even if he had lived through the first attack he would not have survived the terrible wounds without her. She kept his legs covered with poultices made from boiled plants and one day disappeared for hours to find a beehive and collect a large supply of honey, which she applied to the open wounds. She was as gentle as possible, but corded muscles along his jaw revealed the agony it caused. He later learned he was not always quiet when sleeping. Moans and cries rang out as he battled one deadly enemy after another in his nightmares.

Within a few days he was able to sit for long periods against the tree, and they began to communicate through the universal sign language that early people used when confronted with strange tongues. He asked her where she came from and why she was at the deserted pyramid.

"I live far to the north," she signed. "I have always wanted to see the temple. My great grandfather was a priest here long before I was born, when there used to be a great city surrounding the pyramid. He left when my grandfather was a young man and brought the family to where I now live. All my life I have heard stories about the magnificent city and its temple. I decided to see it for myself."

"And what have you found?"

"The last people must have moved away years ago and the temple is all that remains."

"What about the city?" Adzul had not noticed buildings in the area.

"I searched for a week before you arrived but it is all gone. Piles of overgrown rocks scattered over a large area are all that remain. It must have truly been a great city."

"Perhaps there was a war." The warrior was only too familiar with the destruction that a victorious army could cause.

"Perhaps. At least I have seen the temple. It must have been beautiful when my great grandfather was here."

"How did you come to rescue me?"

"I had just returned to camp. We are close to the pyramid here, and I heard the jaguar roar. From the sounds, I knew it was in a fight so I grabbed my spears and ran toward the noise. When I arrived, I saw it was about to kill you. There was no time to lose. My atlatl is powerful at close range and it was so intent on you, I was able to throw the spears from 5 feet away. Both went through its body, but the second one found its heart. The other cat must have been drawn to us by the smell of blood from your wounds."

"You saved my life twice!"

"No." She smiled. "The first time, that shirt saved you! If the jaguar's claws hadn't locked in the fiber, you would have been dead before I arrived. When I took it off, I was amazed there were no wounds on your body!"

"It's a special armor shirt," Adzul explained. "For some reason, I felt a strong urge to put it on before entering the temple."

The girl nodded. "You were wise to heed the feeling!"

CHAPTER 24

Spared!

THE PHONE RANG Sunday evening, just as Great Grandfather was getting ready for bed. It was Sophia. "We just got back from Denver and I've got something amazing to tell you! Can we come over?" The excitement in her voice was compelling.

"Of course, but you must be tired from the trip."

The kids had gone to Denver late Friday to celebrate their birthday at a Colorado Rockies baseball game on Saturday afternoon. It was the first season for the major league team, and the whole family had become fans. Dad and Mom surprised Juan and Sophia with first base line tickets a week earlier, and the twins had been talking about nothing else for the past eight days!

"No way! You've got to hear this!" Sophia was not going to be denied.

"Well, you had better get over here then." The old man couldn't imagine what she was so excited about.

In less than three minutes, there was a knock on the door.

"Holy cow! You weren't kidding!" Great Grandfather spotted their bikes on the lawn. "It must be important if you used bikes to come a block and a half! Come on in, I made peanut butter cookies this afternoon."

Sophia could barely contain herself until a big plate of cookies and glasses of milk were set on the kitchen table. She didn't even wait to bite into her favorite kind of cookie before bursting out.

"You're not going to believe this!"

"Why don't you try me?" Great Grandfather had a twinkle in his eye.

"OK. We're at the game. Second row along the first base line, bottom of the ninth inning."

"The stadium was jammed," Juan interrupted. "Everyone was standing, waving white towels and shouting! It was crazy!"

"The score was 4–7 against a team no one expected the Rockies to beat, but they had loaded the bases and one of their sluggers was coming to bat. There were two outs, so this was their last chance!" The girl leaned forward intently. "The first pitch was a fastball that caught the outside corner of the plate for a strike. The batter swung at the next pitch: strike two. He then let the next three pitches go by for balls so the count is now full, three balls and two strikes." She turned to Juan. "You tell."

"I was at the left end of our seats, Dad and Mom were in the middle, and Sophia was on the right end. At this point, everyone in the stadium was on their feet screaming for a hit! The noise was deafening! I looked down the seats at Sophia and she was jumping up and down, yelling at the top of her lungs! The next pitch was a high fastball and the batter swung with all his might, but he hit the ball on the narrow part of the handle and the bat shattered! The broken bat flew like a missile straight at us. Everyone in the seats along the first base line ducked except Sophia. The jagged end of the bat hit her full force in the chest, like a spear thrown at point-blank range! The impact catapulted her backward onto the floor of the row behind us!

"In an instant the whole stadium went dead quiet, then pandemonium broke loose in our section. Attendants came rushing down the aisles and men and women were scrambling to reach her, but Dad vaulted over the seats and got to her first. I thought she might be seriously injured, or even dead, because the part that hit her was about 8 inches long and sharply pointed! No one could come away from that stabbing without a terrible wound.

"The next thing I see is Sophia standing up and handing the bat to Dad, asking him what she should do with it! Dad's holding her by the shoulders and staring hard at her, asking if she's all right. She's nodding and smiling; the whole crowd suddenly begins to cheer! There's a big rip in her T-shirt, and under it I see gray. It suddenly it dawns on me that she's wearing the armor shirt!

"I heard people around us start asking each other how this girl could possibly be OK, when the batter hits the next pitch out of the park for a grand slam homerun! Everyone forgot about Sophia and went nuts over the Rockies winning the game!"

His sister was now munching a cookie. "I can't explain it Great Grandfather, but Saturday morning I felt a strong urge to wear my armor shirt. I couldn't shake the idea, so I finally gave in and put it on. It seemed so silly to wear it for a baseball game, but it was exactly what I needed! How do you explain that?"

Their relative fixed them with a steady gaze. "I'm certain that it has to do with the medallion. Do you remember back in June I told you the medallion possesses a great secret, and that I thought you two might be the ones to discover it?"

Sophia nodded. "Yes, because we are the first ones in the history of the family who have ever seen through it into the past."

"If you are to unlock the secret, it must involve both of you since you are twins. Somehow you were guided to wear the shirt that day for protection. That's the only explanation I have."

CHAPTER 25
The Mask

THE GIRL'S NAME WAS ITTA. She was curious about Adzul's home, and when he described the years of war with the conquistadors she nodded.

"My father has told me of such men. Once he traveled far to the east, intending to visit Tenochtitlan where our Emperor ruled, only to find the great city in subjection and the population living in terror of these men. Fortunately he was able to make his way back home undetected, but he has always warned our village to be on alert for these soldiers."

"They will stop at nothing to find gold." The warrior's face was grim. "They are deadly enemies."

As Adzul's wounds healed, they taught each other their respective languages and were soon conversing easily. Itta explained that she was Aztec and they wondered how the Spanish had appeared in both empires, which were so far apart, at almost the same time. As they talked, she was constantly working on a piece of jaguar skin — softening, stretching, and sewing it. One day she handed it to him. It was the beautifully preserved skin from the head and neck of the animal that she had killed in their camp.

He was curious. "What is it for?"

"Pull it over your head." She grinned with a mischievous look in her eyes.

To his astonishment, it was a mask that completely covered his head and neck and reached to the top of his chest. The mouth had been sewn shut, but the eyeholes fit him perfectly. She had even stitched the ears down, so the mask gave the appearance of an angry cat with its ears flattened back on its head!

She laughed. "The next time you are attacked, just put on the head skin and the jaguar will be so startled that he will run away! I have even made you a leather sack to keep it protected."

He smiled. "The poor animal won't know whether I am man or beast!"

Itta was fascinated when he told her about the medallion — how it warned him of danger and how it had burned through the ropes that bound him without harming his skin. She examined the strange markings cut into its surface, commenting that it was lighter than Aztec jewelry of the same size.

"It must be very important to have magic like that," she mused.

When he was finally able to walk, they made preparations for the trip north to Itta's village. He had told her about his father's dying instructions, and she invited him to return with her.

"We are the type of friendly people that he told you to settle with."

He was well aware of surging emotions every time he looked at her and quickly accepted the invitation. When they left the little campsite that had been their home for weeks, each was shouldering a sack filled with fruit and dried meat. Adzul's legs had long white scars standing out starkly in his brown skin. As they passed the pyramid, they noticed the vegetation now hid almost every sign of rock.

"Before long it will look like a green hill and no one will know what is there." The girl paused on the trader's path. "I'm glad I saw it before it disappeared."

A month later, they left the trade route and began making their way west. One afternoon they emerged from the forest onto an open hillside. The lowering sun cast a shimmer across a vast expanse of blue stretching away to a distant horizon. Birds circled over waves breaking onto white beaches far below. The tall grass at their feet waved in a gentle breeze.

Adzul's eyes widened at the scene. "Only once have I ever seen such water! When I was a small child, my father took me to the western edge of the mountains and there I saw it. I remember thinking that our lake at home was like a rain puddle by comparison!"

"My village is close to the edge of the water," Itta replied. "We're almost home!"

The following afternoon they descended the hills and came to cultivated fields. In the distance, a cluster of flat-roofed white houses marked the village. People working in the fields stopped to watch their approach. The men wore the same cotton shirt and pants that Itta did, but the women's shirts had colorful designs sewn into them. As they recognized the girl, hands were raised and greetings shouted accompanied by stares of curiosity at the Incan warrior striding beside her.

When they reached the village, consisting of a short street with one-story houses on either side, a buzz of excitement went through the Aztecs mingled there for trade and barter. Itta had been gone for several months, and many thought she must have died in an accident. Amid the welcoming shouts a woman broke through the crowd and dashed up to embrace her in a bear hug, tears running freely down her cheeks. Itta returned the hug, laughing happily, and they held on to each other for several minutes oblivious of the crowd that had gathered! When they finally broke apart Itta introduced her mother to Adzul, describing what had happened with such an outpouring of words that he could barely follow what she was saying. The older woman stared at the scars on his legs.

"Your daughter saved my life three times," he said. "Twice she killed jaguars with her spears, and her expert care healed the wounds that would otherwise have killed me! I owe her my life."

When Itta's mother saw the look that passed between Adzul and the girl she knew there was more than gratitude in his heart, and she immediately warmed to the handsome warrior.

"You must stay with us," she said. "I have salve that will help with your legs."

She led the way to their house where Adzul met Tlaloc and Quauhtli, Itta's father and 15-year-old brother. A meal was prepared, and the Incan was offered vegetables wrapped in tortillas. He held the cylinder of food in his hands, uncertain how to eat it.

"Do you have this food where you come from?" Her father noticed that the warrior was waiting for the rest of them to eat before attempting it.

"Not exactly," Adzul said. "We eat bread made from maize, but it is not wrapped around food this way. In the mountains we have soup of potatoes, dried meat, and maize. But I am familiar with those." He pointed to the rows of peppers hanging from the ceiling. "We use them in all our cooking."

"Let me show you," Tlaloc said kindly. He tipped the tortilla up and took a bite from one end, quickly returning it to a horizontal position before any food could run out of the opening he had made.

"I see!" Adzul caught on and was soon eating tortillas with as much enthusiasm as if they had been his favorite food since childhood!

Life soon settled into a routine for Adzul in the community. Itta's family spent almost every day in their garden at the outskirts of the town. The Incan warrior had never farmed before but he was eager to learn everything he could, and the chance to work alongside Itta for hours was irresistible! In addition, he proved invaluable at providing the household with a continuous supply of fresh meat. He was a natural hunter and roamed the nearby hills in pursuit of rabbits, birds, and deer. Itta and Quauhtli usually went with him and were amazed at his skill with the sling.

"He can hit a bird in flight!" the boy announced one night to an astonished Tlaloc.

Adzul was equally impressed with their use of the atlatl. Tlaloc had started both of them throwing spears when they were small, and their accuracy was marvelous. When practicing, they would repeatedly put the spear through an avocado 30 yards away!

CHAPTER 26

Grapefruit

THE INCAN WAS particularly interested in Tlaloc's experience with the conquistadors.

"Itta told me you once encountered them," he mentioned one night. "Did they have horses?"

"Yes," the older man replied. "We had never seen such animals and after we recovered from our fear, we realized what an advantage they gave the enemy. I saw several mounted men attack and quickly defeat a group of Aztec warriors that greatly outnumbered them."

Adzul nodded. "We fought them many times. In the beginning our men were also scared of the horses, but we developed strategies to deal with them. Have the soldiers ever come here?"

"No. We are removed from the main trade routes, and not many people know our location. We are a small village of farmers, which is unlikely to arouse their interest."

"We believed the same thing in our land; however, when they had finished searching the cities they spread out into the countryside. Lust for gold drives them everywhere! If they come upon you here, the ocean offers no escape; they will massacre everyone before you can flee to the concealment of the jungle."

Tlaloc was somber. "When I first returned from Tenochtitlan years ago, I was scared the enemy would find us. I advised our headman to establish lookout posts several miles away to give us time to flee to the hills if they appeared. For a while we manned the lookouts, but after years of quiet they were abandoned. There's another Aztec village 10 miles away, and we rely on them to warn us."

Adzul was not confident about this arrangement, but he said nothing.

The only jarring note to life with the Aztecs was the presence of Yaoti, a tall and rather serious young man who began to appear at the garden every day to see Itta. He completely ignored Adzul and hung around the girl until the day's work was done. Itta didn't encourage him, but neither did she discourage him! Finally, the Incan questioned her brother.

"Oh, that's Yaoti," said Quauhtli. "He's planning to marry Itta."

"How long has he known her?" Adzul tried not to show his surprise.

"They grew up together, of course." Quauhtli cast a sharp look at the Incan.

"Is he a good man?" The warrior kept his tone of voice neutral.

"Why do you ask?" The boy began to get a smile on his face.

"Your sister saved my life. She's worthy of a good man for her husband."

"You're entirely right. I just wondered why you are so interested in him." Quauhtli pretended innocence.

"What do you mean?" But the warrior averted his eyes.

"Oh, nothing." The boy turned away with a grin.

When it became apparent that Itta was seriously interested in Adzul, Yaoti became sullen and refused to acknowledge the Incan. He even brushed past him roughly in the street. To make matters worse, he started to voice derogatory comments about Adzul to other men in the village. After weeks of this behavior, Adzul decided to bring the matter to a head.

One afternoon when Yaoti was talking to a group of men in the village, the warrior asked Quauhtli to get a grapefruit. He told the boy to move 25 yards down the street and place the grapefruit on top of his head. Adzul unwrapped the sling from his waist and loaded it. When Quauhtli was in position, the warrior motioned people out of the way and started swinging the weapon. Conversation ceased as the hum of the straps filled the air. All eyes were fixed on Adzul and when he released the rock, its speed was so great that people could barely see it. What they did see was the grapefruit on Quauhtli's head suddenly explode in a thousand pieces!

A loud exclamation went up from the villagers. Men's eyes widened and women's hands flew up to their mouths in astonishment. Although they had heard rumors about his skill, no one except Itta and Quauhtli had seen him throw. A shout of enthusiasm went up from the men as Yaoti dropped his eyes and walked away. From that time on, he began courting another young woman in the village.

A week later, Adzul and Itta walked near the ocean as the sun was going down. The great orange globe appeared to be slowly sliding into the sea far away at the horizon. Just offshore, the dorsal fins of a dolphin pod dipped in and out of the smooth water as they cruised in search of food. Seagulls dived overhead with raucous calls, hoping the couple might have a morsel for them, while on the beach a huge sea turtle made its unhurried way to the high-tide line to lay its eggs that night. As they stood quietly gazing at the tranquil scene, Adzul asked Itta to marry him. With tears of joy, she accepted.

CHAPTER 27

The Wedding

PREPARATIONS FOR THE wedding went forward, and everyone in the village was pleased. Tlaloc's family was well regarded, and Adzul had become a favorite in the four months since he arrived. Even Yaoti had to admit the Incan worked as hard as anyone, and he was the most skilled hunter in the community. He finally stopped Adzul one day to congratulate him and to mention that one of Itta's best friends had captured his own heart. From that time forward, the two men became close friends.

Finally the day came. The wedding took place in the late afternoon at a house that had been provided for the couple. Adzul and Itta sat side by side on a mat especially woven for the occasion by several of the women. Itta was radiant with colorful flowers in her black hair and a necklace of blossoms around her neck; Adzul could not take his eyes off of her!

The house was crowded with people as Itta's mother placed a new blouse on the mat in front of Itta and a new cotton shirt in front of Adzul. Following the Aztec custom, she slowly tied the sleeves of the two garments together in a knot, signifying the couple was bound together in marriage. When she had finished, everyone shouted their approval and moved outside for a feast!

As dusk fell, torches were lit and the area in front of the house filled with people talking and eating. The newlyweds sat on their mat in front of the door and received gifts of food, clothing, and other items to help start their new life together. A full moon was well up in the sky when an unknown man suddenly stumbled out of the darkness into the torchlight and fell face forward on the ground. Dried blood covered his head and his clothes were in tatters.

There was stunned silence as Adzul leaped from the mat and gently lifted the man to a sitting position. His scalp was split from the top of his head to his left ear, and he appeared to have been stabbed in the chest.

"Water!" cried the Incan, using his shirt to wipe blood from the man's face. Someone grabbed a gourd and passed it to Adzul. Splashing water on the man's face, he held the gourd for him to drink.

The man's eyelids fluttered and then snapped open. "Flee!" he croaked. "They're coming!" As the water cleared his throat, he stared with wild eyes at Adzul and yelled. "I'm the last one. They killed everyone else! They're coming!"

"I know him!" one of the men in the crowd exclaimed. "He's a farmer from the next village!"

In a calm voice, Adzul asked, "How many men were there and when did this happen?"

"Early this afternoon. There were 20 men on horses, and they attacked without warning. We never had a chance; they killed everyone on sight, including the children. I don't think anyone escaped!" Tears ran from his eyes. "They thought I was dead, and I managed to escape in the dark. I came to warn you." He passed out.

"Take him into the house and tend to his wounds," Adzul ordered. Several men stepped forward and gently picked up the stranger while women ran to get bandages and water.

The Incan turned to the headman. "We need to act immediately!"

"You're the one who has fought them. What do you suggest?" The man's voice was calm, but his eyes showed fear.

Adzul spoke rapidly. "My experience tells me they will get drunk and celebrate at the village tonight, sleeping well into the morning tomorrow. When they have pulled themselves together they will start along the path toward us and arrive in the midafternoon, expecting to take us by surprise. We should send all the women, children, and older people into the hills immediately and prepare for battle."

"Why don't we all flee?" one of the men asked.

The warrior looked him in the eye. "They will follow us into the hills and massacre everyone. We need to make a stand in the village, where we have the advantage of surprise."

Tlaloc spoke. "Adzul is right. I have seen these men. I know they have no mercy and will kill every one of us if given the chance. We need to fight to save our families."

Adzul glanced at his father-in-law. "More than just fight," he said softly.

The headman looked at the Incan warrior. "We will do as you direct."

CHAPTER 28

Evacuation

Under Adzul's direction, plans were made to evacuate the village. Excluding six women, he set everyone to work assembling all of the food, clothing, farming tools, chickens, and baby geese that could be carried or packed on dogs. Domesticated geese and turkeys were turned loose in the hills and everything that could not be carried was buried in the gardens. The village was to be completely cleaned out, for Adzul had no intention of letting the people return.

The six women were directed to collect many blankets and cut them into thin 3-foot strips. When this was finished, they assembled at his house where young boys had gathered a large pile of fist-sized rocks.

He showed the women how to tie three lengths of cloth together at one end and to attach a rock to each of the other ends. The result was a bola: a three-stranded, weighted weapon that could be thrown through the air like a revolving helicopter blade. It was to be used against the horses.

The villagers worked with urgent efficiency. Within four hours they had stripped every house of its contents and packed what could be carried, burying the rest in the soft dirt of the gardens. By midnight the town looked abandoned, and the fleeing group was ready to leave. Six of the older boys and 18 men were staying.

The six women had made 36 bolas. Adzul thanked them, and they joined the others to get their packs. Itta, who had been helping, remained on the floor.

"I'm not leaving." she declared.

"You must," he said. "These villagers are farmers, not warriors, and there is a good chance we will all die. The women and children will need your skills to survive."

"We were only married this afternoon!" Her eyes flashed. "I will not leave you, not after all we've been through. If you die here, so will I! Besides, my spears may be useful in the fighting."

The warrior sighed. "Very well, but I wish you weren't so stubborn." The love in his eyes, however, revealed his joy that she was staying.

"It's settled then!" she cried, jumping to her feet and giving him a long kiss. "I need to say goodbye to my mother and prepare my weapons!"

Under the light of the full moon, a large group assembled at the edge of the village. Everyone carried a pack of some kind, even the children, and two of the younger women carried the wounded neighbor on a litter. Mothers slung babies across their chests and bundles of food and clothing on their backs. Every dog in the village was strapped with a load, and even the elderly people carried light packs.

Goodbyes were quickly made amid the tears of many women who feared they would never see their husbands and sons again. One of the old men who had been a trader in his youth was directed to lead the group north, keeping clear of known trails.

"In the beginning stay on hard ground so you won't leave tracks, but after a day move as fast as you can and don't worry about making a trail. By then distance will become your most important ally. Keep walking and don't send anyone back to look for us, even if many days go by; we will find you after we have dealt with the raiders." Adzul left unspoken a grim warning. If the conquistadors killed him and his little band, and then discovered someone returning to the scene, they would track down the remaining villagers like a pack of rabid dogs.

The old trader's eyes revealed that he understood. "We will go far to the north beyond the outposts of the Empire and wait for you."

Adzul and Itta, with 24 men and boys, watched the group march out of sight in the moonlight before they returned to the houses for a few hours of sleep.

As Adzul arranged the bolas against one wall in their house, he spoke ruefully. "This isn't the way I imagined our wedding would end."

"We're together and that's all that matters." Itta smiled and came into his arms.

CHAPTER 29

Cougar!

THE HAIR ON THE BACK of Juan's neck began to prickle. "Something's wrong," he whispered to Sophia sitting beside him.

"I feel it too," she murmured.

"The medallion is beginning to get hot!" he gasped.

It was a beautiful fall afternoon in the San Juan Mountains, and they were engaged in one of their most favorite activities of the year: locating elk with Dad for the upcoming hunting season. Since middle school sporting events were generally held on weekdays, they were able to leave with Dad on Friday afternoon and spend two days camping and trekking high ridgelines in search of the wary animals.

They loved it because Dad often used his elk call to lure a big bull close to where they were hiding in the trees. Thinking it was being challenged to a fight by another elk, the bull sometimes approached within a few yards thrashing small trees with its antlers in rage! As long as they remained motionless, dressed in their camouflage clothing, it couldn't spot them unless it caught their scent. If that happened it was gone in a flash! They were always amazed that such a big animal could disappear through the forest so quickly and quietly.

At the moment, they were seated under a spruce tree at the bottom of a cliff high on a ridge. Behind them was a jumble of large boulders that had broken off the cliff during past centuries. In front, and far below, was a valley with big meadows onto which elk would emerge at twilight to spend the night feeding. The twins were armed with high-powered binoculars for spotting big bulls among the grazing animals. Dad was several hundred yards to the south watching a different area of the meadows.

It was late afternoon when the feeling of danger hit. Neither moved, their eyes searching the few scattered trees for the cause of their uneasiness. The slope around them was steep and covered with pine needles and outcrops of rock, but the lack of trees gave them an unobstructed view. Nothing appeared out of the ordinary, but Juan could not shake the sensation that there was a threat.

"Did you notice the squirrel has stopped chattering?" He kept his voice low.

"Yes, and the chickadees have all disappeared."

"Better get the slings out," he whispered, beginning to unwrap the weapon from his waist.

Sophia nodded and followed suit. From the leather pouch at her waist she selected a smooth rock and armed the sling.

"Let's slowly stand up, keeping our backs to the tree." Juan jerked his head to the side. "I think the danger is behind us."

He gradually rose to his full height, keeping his back to the tree, with Sophia copying him on the right. They slowly moved their heads around either side of the trunk to study the boulder field behind. For a minute, all seemed normal.

"There it is!" The boy gave a sharp intake of breath.

Sophia saw it at the same instant: a large mountain lion crouched on a boulder above them 30 feet away. Its ears were flat back on its head, and they could just see the twitching of its long tail behind.

"It's getting ready to jump," she muttered.

The twins had been well schooled by their father about what to do when encountering one of the big cats. They were to stand with their arms stretched high, preferably spreading a jacket above their heads, so as to appear as large as possible. They were to pretend aggression by shouting and taking a step or two forward.

"Usually that intimidates the lion and it will turn away," Dad explained. "Never, never, run away. The cat will be on you in an instant like a tabby after a mouse!"

"Jump around the tree and stand beside me and raise your arms," Juan directed. "Standing together, we should make a pretty big figure."

When they were in position with up-raised arms, both began shouting as loudly as they could but the cat only slid back a couple of feet, its tail lashing furiously.

"It's wounded!" exclaimed Sophia. "I saw big cuts and dried blood along the ribs when it moved."

"Maybe it attacked a bull elk and got hurt enough that it can't catch a deer. It certainly isn't backing off."

When the animal crept back to the front of the boulder, Juan knew it wasn't going to leave.

"We'd better separate and get the slings going."

The sudden motion of the kids stepping away from each other, and the hum of the slings, seemed to confuse the mountain lion. It backed up a few feet but quickly advanced again to the edge of the boulder, and let out a blood-curdling snarl!

"It's going to jump!" shouted Juan. "I'll throw first!"

Without waiting for an answer, he threw the rock with the full force of the 5-foot sling. It struck the cat just below the eye on the left side of its face, and the kids clearly heard bone break. The animal let out an unearthly scream and sprang at the boy, just as a heavy rock released by Sophia slammed into it at more than 100 miles per hour and broke its shoulder blade.

The lion hit the ground 8 feet from Juan and rolled over and over before fetching up against a small tree. It crouched there on three legs snarling horribly at them, but it was unable to charge.

Both slings were whirling again when they heard shouts and knew Dad was coming. They saw him running across the slope as fast as he could. When he arrived, he took the scene in at a glance and reached for the powerful revolver on his belt.

Upon examining the dead cat, they discovered that the antlers of an elk had indeed seriously wounded it.

"See the spacing of those rips in its skin?" Dad explained. "That old bull probably caught it in midair with a horrific swipe of its antlers, and I'm surprised it didn't stomp it to death before it escaped! It's pretty thin. You were right to take action, son; this one wasn't going to stop until he got one or the other of you!"

Juan and Sophia looked at each other. "Never stop practicing." They spoke in perfect unison, reciting the words of Great Grandfather.

CHAPTER 30

The Trap

Well before the sun rose, Adzul had the boys throwing bolas at small trees. They soon became adept at releasing the weapon with enough force so the weight of the rocks caused all three strands to wrap around the trunk. Quauhtli had a knack for it because he had spent time learning to use the sling, and he understood the throwing motion.

The Incan encouraged them. "If you can be accurate under pressure this afternoon, it will be a key to our success."

They redoubled their efforts, competing to see who could strike the tree every time between 8 and

10 inches above the ground: the ideal height to ensnare the legs of a horse.

The men went to work building a hedge of brush 5-feet high on either side of the track coming into town. This corridor, 70-yards long and 30-feet wide, would have to be traveled by the riders to reach the houses. The flat roof of the first house on the right was stacked with a supply of spears for Itta's atlatl. The house across the street had a similar supply of rocks for Adzul's sling. When the work was complete, everyone spent the rest of the morning sharpening the blades of knives, hatchets, and hoes to a razor's edge.

When the preparations were finished, Adzul addressed the group. "These men are trained soldiers, but they will be arrogant and confident after the victory yesterday and think they are coming to another village that will offer no resistance — one they can easily plunder and burn. To defeat them we must strike with shock and surprise, never giving them the chance to get organized."

His next words were slow and forceful. "Not one of them can be allowed to escape."

In the dead silence that followed, his voice left no room for misunderstanding. "If even one escapes, we are doomed! A large force will return with vengeance and track us down until they have killed every man, woman, and child."

He then outlined the strategy. The boys with bolas were to be stationed between the houses on either side of the street. Quauhtli would be at the last house because his would be the first bola launched, signaling the rest of them to throw. Four of the most skilled archers were assigned to rooftops from which they could cover the entire length of the street. All the other men were to hide between the houses, ready to spring into the street wielding an assortment of weapons. He emphasized that no one was to show himself until the first bolas were thrown.

"The Spaniards are good fighters. When the horses go down, you must instantly attack and prevent any soldier from remounting; a mounted man is worth five men on foot! Show no mercy; it would be better to die than suffer their tortures if we fail. Itta and I will try to prevent anyone from escaping down the corridor."

With grim faces, the men and boys scattered to their positions.

After making sure that Itta was well concealed on her roof, Adzul gave her a lingering kiss.

"Be careful, I don't want to lose you now," he whispered in her ear.

"Be careful yourself," she replied, holding him tight. "I have no intention of losing you after less than one day of marriage!"

He put on his armor shirt and returned to the ground, studying the street. Everyone was so well hidden that it looked completely deserted. Satisfied, he walked down the brush corridor and along the path into the grassland where he found a shady bush to sit under. The sun was hot and for an hour the only sound was the cheerful singing of meadowlarks swooping over the grasses.

CHAPTER 31

Battle

A~T THE SAME MOMENT~ that Adzul heard the clink of armor, he felt vibration in the ground from the hooves of horses. Peering around the bush, he saw a lazy cloud of dust rising above the trail. He knew his lookouts in the village could see it and were alerting the men. The soldiers came into sight just 300 yards away. There were 20 of them riding two abreast, led by the commander on a black horse. All were laughing and talking with complete disregard for the noise they were making. Armed with swords and lances, the group included two men carrying the blunderbusses he had seen before.

When the column was 50 yards away, Adzul burst from behind the bushes and ran a few steps toward them, sling whirling. Instinctively, the captain reined in his horse and signaled with his arm for the column to stop while he assessed the situation. Without warning a hurtling rock struck him squarely on the point of the chin, shattering his jaw! A scream of pain filled the air and the captain's face contorted with fury. Pulling his sword, he savagely spurred his horse in pursuit of the warrior who was already fleeing, the entire column behind him surging to a run.

Adzul sprinted down the corridor, but the running horses quickly ate up his lead. Two men had already passed the captain and were rapidly gaining, eager to avenge their leader and possibly earn a reward for their effort. The rest were in a pack close behind; their blood lust aroused in anticipation of slaughtering the entire village.

When the flying warrior reached the first houses, the thundering horses were only 15 yards behind and closing the gap with every jump! Sweat covered his face as he ran like he had never run before, arms pumping frantically at his sides. Suddenly he realized that he had underestimated the horses' speed, and he was not sure he could make it to the house where Quauhtli waited. The adobe walls were a blur on either side as he felt the horses thundering down on him.

In horror, the hidden Aztecs saw the lead rider drop the tip of his lance and lean forward to stab the running man in the leg, intending to trample him as he fell. The blade was inches from Adzul's calf as he flashed past the alley where his brother-in-law waited, arm swinging the bola. Quauhtli flung the weighted weapon with all his strength just before the lance touched the Incan's leg. The perfectly thrown bola wrapped itself around the front legs of the horse, causing it to pitch forward head over heals. It happened so fast the rider was helpless to avoid the animal's body crashing down on him. His back was snapped with an audible 'crack!'

Simultaneously, the other boys let fly at the racing column and the street erupted in a tangle of screaming horses and men. The horses at the end of the line were tripped by bolas and catapulted end over end onto the struggling mass of bodies in front of them! The animals landing on conquistadors broke the mens' ribs, shoulders, legs, and hips. Soldiers who survived the fall were dealt crippling blows by the hooves of frantic horses trying to fight their way upright and out of the melee.

Into this bedlam the Aztecs charged like maniacs swinging hatchets, knives, and hoes. The latter were particularly effective because they could be swung with great force from 2- or 3-feet away, delivering terrible wounds. The villagers went about their work with deadly efficiency, determined to let none escape. Many soldiers never regained their feet before being hacked down. A few managed to stand and fight for their lives, only to receive an arrow deep in the throat from one of the archers above.

As Adzul passed Quauhtli he dodged suddenly to the left, fearing that the falling horses would crush him. Gasping for breath, he darted behind the houses and ran to the head of the street with the screams of men and horses filling his ears. He raced up the ladder to the roof and grabbed his loaded sling, eyes searching the street below.

Directly beneath him, Yaoti was in a desperate struggle with the captain who had miraculously turned his horse and spurred to escape the ambush. The Aztec had charged from cover and somehow dragged him off the horse with his bare hands. But the captain was a skilled fighter despite his broken jaw and slashed Yaoti across the chest with his sword, knocking him to the ground. Raising the sword overhead with both hands, he was about to cleave Yaoti's skull when Itta's spear entered his stomach just below the armor chest plate and emerged out his back. Dropping the sword, he gripped the shaft of the spear and stumbled backwards. A shocked look came over his face as he slowly fell on his side, feet drawn up under him.

Another soldier stumbled out of the dust and dropped to his knees beside Yaoti, who was struggling to rise. Grabbing a fistful of black hair, he tipped the Aztec's head back to cut his throat. But the knife fell from his lifeless hand as a rock from Adzul's sling smashed into his skull above the right ear! Leaping from the roof, the Incan raced to Yaoti and dragged him to safety behind the house. Quickly binding the wound with strips torn from his cotton shirt, he spoke urgently.

"Hang on, the fight isn't over yet. I'll be back for you!" Yaoti nodded his thanks as his friend dashed away.

CHAPTER 32

Reunion

THE BATTLE ENDED as quickly as it started. Adzul's strategy had worked perfectly. The few soldiers who emerged unhurt from the wreckage of tumbling horses had been quickly dispatched. The others had been so badly injured they offered little resistance. So fierce had been the attack, the fight was over in 10 minutes!

Itta leaped from her roof and hugged her husband. "I was terrified they would run you over before you reached Quauhtli!" she cried.

He smiled through the sweat and dirt covering his face and held her closely. "I overestimated my speed and the horses were faster than I remembered!"

She smiled. "You saved Yaoti's life!"

"As did you. Now we can all look forward to his wedding!"

Quauhtli came running. "Did you have to make it so close? I was certain they were going to lance you, and I've never thrown anything so hard in my life!"

Adzul put his arms around both of them. "I'm glad you were ready when I got there because there was no more speed in these legs! Now, let's look after our wounded."

To his amazement, their casualties were light. No one had been killed, but two men had broken their arms when they waded into the melee of bodies and were kicked by horses. Several others had received sword wounds from soldiers before help arrived. One man had had lost an ear to a sword but proudly announced that his assailant had lost his life to a hoe!

Yaoti's chest was bleeding profusely, and he needed immediate help. A fire was quickly built and used to heat the blade of a Spanish sword until it glowed. While five men held Yaoti down Adzul applied the red-hot steel to the wound, cauterizing it to stop the bleeding. Yaoti mercifully passed out before Adzul was finished. Then Itta took over and applied salves and bandages.

"He's going to have a big scar, but I think he will recover completely," she announced.

After making certain none of the conquistadors remained alive, the group moved well away from the houses for the night. Everyone was exhausted from the emotional and physical ferocity of the battle, and no one wanted to stay at the scene. Yaoti was laid down and covered with a blanket. The rest of the wounded were treated, and by sunset the entire party was asleep in a grove of trees.

The next morning, they set to work removing all evidence of the battle. The surviving horses were used to drag the dead ones far into the hills where predators would devour them. The soldiers, along with their saddles and equipment, were buried in a deep ravine and covered with dirt and boulders to keep wild beasts away.

Adzul then implemented the final step of his strategy. The gardens were dug up and covered with brush and dead tree limbs, and the wooden beams of the houses were set on fire so that the roofs would collapse. Every shred of evidence that people had recently lived there was removed. The brush corridor was taken down and its material scattered throughout the village, from which all footprints were swept away. It took several days, but when they finished the town looked like it hadn't been occupied for years!

Quauhtli was puzzled. "Surely they will come looking for these soldiers?"

Adzul smiled grimly. "We learned the conquistador leaders were almost as cruel to their own men as they were to the Incans. Many soldiers fled when they had a chance; perhaps the commanders will think this group deserted. If a patrol is sent, it will be weeks before they arrive and they will only find ruins being taken over by the jungle. There will be nothing to suggest anyone has lived here for years, or that the command had ever been here!"

Rounding up the horses they set off into the hills, carefully brushing away all traces of their passing. Many miles away, they released the horses into a lush valley. Ten days later, they caught up with the rest of the villagers. True to his word the old trader had led them far to the north, walking from dawn to dusk every day. Joyous reunions erupted as men and boys rejoined their families, often tossing little ones high in the air to delighted squeals. In the midst of it a beautiful girl who could have been Itta's twin clung to Yaoti, sobbing with relief and happiness.

Weeks later, the old trader led them through a range of hills into a beautiful valley filled with grasslands. It was encompassed by forested hills and a small river meandered through it, flanked by groves of cottonwood trees. Herds of deer were feeding in meadows of rich grass, and a hawk spiraled in the air looking for prey.

Their guide looked thoughtfully at the scene. "When I was a young man, I traveled many days to the west of the trade routes looking for a village that was supposed to be in these hills. The village did not exist, but I came upon this valley. I remember thinking at the time that it would be a wonderful place to settle."

And so it was.

The Heirs of the Medallion
Cuto
Book 2

EIGHTY YEARS AFTER Adzul and Itta settle in their new home, their grandson Cuto inherits the medallion. Bored with life in the peaceful farming village, he and his young wife head north to seek adventure in a new community named Santa Fe. The journey is filled with danger and they arrive to find the area controlled by conquistadors, the nemesis of the Aztec.

They quickly realize that, on foot, they and the local Pueblo Indians are no match for the mounted soldiers. Cuto comes up with a daring plan to help the Indians but is forced to flee to a secret desert canyon, where he and Ria begin a new life.

As their whereabouts become known, new threats arise and only the medallion stands between Cuto and the loss of everything he loves.

CPSIA information can be obtained at www.ICGtesting.com
Printed in the USA
BVOW07s1626251113

337289BV00001B/1/P